It isn't true what they say about your life passing before you. You're too busy. You're at it full time, bashing at the water with your arms and screaming "Help!" to nothing and nobody. And too busy keeping afloat. I hadn't the least idea how to swim. What I did was a sort of crazy jumping up and down, standing in the water, with miles more water down underneath me, bending and stretching like a mad frog, and it kept me up. It also turned me round in a circle. Every way was water, with sky at the end of it. Nothing in sight at all, except flaring sunlit water on one side and heaving gray water on the other.

Also by Diana Wynne Jones

Archer's Goon
Aunt Maria
Believing Is Seeing: Seven Stories
Castle in the Air
Dark Lord of Derkholm
Dogsbody
Eight Days of Luke
Fire and Hemlock
Hexwood
Hidden Turnings: A Collection of Stories Through Time and Space
Howl's Moving Castle
The Ogre Downstairs
Power of Three
Stopping for a Spell
A Tale of Time City
The Time of the Ghost
Warlock at the Wheel and Other Stories
Year of the Griffin

THE WORLDS OF CHRESTOMANCI
Book 1: Charmed Life
Book 2: The Lives of Christopher Chant
Book 3: The Magicians of Caprona
Book 4: Witch Week
Mixed Magics: Four Tales of Chrestomanci
The Chronicles of Chrestomanci, Volume 1 (Contains books 1 and 2)
The Chronicles of Chrestomanci, Volume 2 (Contains books 3 and 4)

THE DALEMARK QUARTET
Book 1: Cart and Cwidder
Book 2: Drowned Ammet
Book 3: The Spellcoats
Book 4: The Crown of Dalemark

Diana Wynne Jones

THE
Homeward
Bounders

A Greenwillow Book

HarperTrophy®
An Imprint of HarperCollins*Publishers*

The Homeward Bounders
Copyright © 1981 by Diana Wynne Jones
All rights reserved. No part of this book may be used or reproduced in
any manner whatsoever without written permission except in the case
of brief quotations embodied in critical articles and reviews. Printed in
the United States of America. For information address HarperCollins
Children's Books, a division of HarperCollins Publishers,
1350 Avenue of the Americas, New York, NY 10019.

Library of Congress Cataloging-in-Publication Data
Jones, Diana Wynne.
  The homeward bounders.
    p.   cm.
  "Greenwillow Books."
  Summary: Once he becomes a pawn in a game played by a powerful
group he calls Them, 12-year-old Jamie is repeatedly catapulted
through space and time.
  ISBN 0-06-029886-3 — ISBN 0-06-447353-8 (pbk.)
  [1. Space and time—Fiction.] I. Title.
PZ7.J684Ho   81-1905
[Fic]   AACR2

◆

First Harper Trophy edition, 2002
Visit us on the World Wide Web!
www.harperteen.com

❖

To Thomas Tuckett,
with thanks for advice
about War Gaming

❖

I

Have you heard of the Flying Dutchman? No? Nor of the Wandering Jew? Well, it doesn't matter. I'll tell you about them in the right place; and about Helen and Joris, Adam and Konstam, and Vanessa, the sister Adam wanted to sell as a slave. They were all Homeward Bounders like me. And I'll tell about *Them* too, who made us that way.

All in good time. I'll tell about this machine I'm talking into first. It's one of *Theirs*. *They* have everything. It has a high piece in front that comes to a neat square with a net over it. You talk into that. As soon as you talk, a little black piece at the back starts hopping and jabbering up and down like an excited idiot, and paper starts rolling over a roller from somewhere underneath. The hopping bit jabbers along the paper, printing out exactly the words you say as fast as you can say them. And it puts in commas and full-stops and things of its own accord. It doesn't seem to worry it what you say. I called it some rude words when I was trying it out, just to see, and it wrote them all down, with exclamation marks after them.

When it's written about a foot of talk, it cuts that off and shoots it out into a tray in front, so that you can read it over, or take it away if you want. And it does this without ever stopping jabbering. If you stop talking, it goes on hopping up and down for a while, in an expectant sort of way, waiting for you to go on. If you don't go on, it slows down and stops, looking sad and disappointed. It put me off at first, doing that. I had to practice with it. I don't like it to stop. The silence creeps in then. I'm the only one in the Place now. Everyone has gone, even him—the one whose name I don't know.

My name is Jamie Hamilton and I was a perfectly ordinary boy once. I am still, in a way. I look about thirteen. But you wouldn't believe how old I am. I was twelve when this happened to me. A year is an awful long time to a Homeward Bounder.

I really enjoyed my twelve years of ordinary life. Home to me is a big city, and always will be. We lived in a really big, dirty, slummy city. The back of our house looked out on to a lovely cosy courtyard, where everyone came out and talked in fine weather, and everyone knew everyone else. The front of our house was our grocery shop, and all the neighbors shopped there. We were open every day, including Sunday. My mother was a bit of a sharp woman. She was always having rows in the courtyard, usually about credit. She used to say the neighbors expected to buy things for nothing just because they lived in the court, and she told them so to their faces. But no one could have been kinder than my mother when a neighbor's daughter was run over by a brewer's wagon. I often hope they were as kind to her over me.

My father was big and soft-spoken and kind all the time. He used to let people buy things for nothing. When my mother objected, he used to say, "Now, Margaret, they needed it." And usually that stopped the argument.

The arguments my father couldn't seem to stop were always over me. The main one was because I was in my last year at school. School cost money. My school cost rather more than my father could afford, because it had pretensions to grandeur. It was called Churt House, and it was in a dreary building like a chapel, and I remember it as if it were yesterday. We had all sorts of pretend-posh customs—like calling our teachers Dominies and a School Song—and that was why my mother liked it.

My mother desperately wanted me to grow up to be something better than a grocer. She was convinced I was clever, and she wanted a doctor in the family. She saw me as a famous surgeon, consulted by Royalty, so she naturally wanted me to stay on at school. My father was dead against it. He said he hadn't the money. He wanted me at home, to help in the shop. They argued about it all the last year I was at home.

Me—I don't know which side I was on. School bored me stiff. All that sitting and learning lists: lists of spelling, lists of tables, lists of History dates, lists of Geography places. I'd rather do anything else, even now, than learn a list. About the only part of school I enjoyed was the feud we had with the really posh school up the road. It was called Queen Elizabeth Academy, and the boys there wore shiny hats and learned music and things. They despised us—rightly—for pretending to be better than we were, and we despised them just as much for the silly hats and the music. We used to have some really good fights on the way home. But the rest of school bored me solid.

On the other hand, the shop bored me almost as much. I'd always rather leave the shop to my brother, Rob. He was younger than me. He thought it was the greatest treat on earth to count change and put up sugar in blue paper bags. My little sister, Elsie, liked the shop too, only she'd always rather play football with me.

Football was the thing I really loved. We used to play in the back alley, between our court and the one behind, our court stick the kids from the other one. That usually boiled down to me and Elsie against the two Macready boys. We were the ones who always played. We had to have special rules because the space was so small, and more special rules for washing days, because people's coppers in the wash-houses on either side filled the whole alley with steam. It was like playing in fog. I was forever landing the ball in someone's washing. That made the other arguments my mother had that my father couldn't settle. She was always having rows about what I'd done with the ball this time, or with Mrs. Macready because I'd led her boys into bad ways. I never was a saint. If it wasn't football, it was something else that was a laugh to do. My mother always tried to stick up for me, but it was a lost cause.

The other thing I used to love was exploring round the city. I used to do it on my way to school, or coming home, so that my mother wouldn't know. This is where *They* come in, so don't get impatient.

That year I was taking a new bit of the city every week and going round it till I knew it. Then I'd move on. I told you a city is Home to me. Most of it was just like it was round our court, crowded and cheery and grimy. But I used to love the market. Everyone shouting like mad, and oranges to nick off every barrow, and big gas flares over all the stalls. I saw one catch fire one time. Then there was the canal and the railway. They used to go out of their way to criss-cross one another, it always seemed to me. Trains were clanking over the water every hundred yards, or else barges were getting dragged under iron bridges—except for one bit, where the canal went over the railway for a change on a line of high arches like stilts, with houses packed underneath the arches. Near that was the smart bit with the good shops. I used to love the smart bit in winter in the dark, when there were lights all wriggling down into the wet road, and posh people in carriages going up and down. Then there were the quiet bits. You'd come upon them suddenly, round a corner—gray, quiet parts that everyone seemed to have forgotten.

The quiet bit that was the end of me was right near the center. It was round behind the smart bit, almost under the place where the canal went up on its stilts. I came at it through a sort of park first. It was a private park. I wasn't particular about trespassing. I suppose you'd call the place a garden. But I was really ignorant in those days. The only other grass I'd seen was in a park, so I thought of this place as a park when I came over the wall into it.

It was a triangular green place. Though it was right in the heart of the city, it had more trees—and bushes—in it than I'd ever seen all together in those days. It creased down to a hollow in the middle, where there was grass, smooth mown grass. The moment I landed over the wall, the quiet shut me in. It was peaceful in a way, but it was more like going deaf. I couldn't hear so much as a whisper from the railway or the roads.

Funny! I thought, and looked up to make sure the canal was still there. And it was there, striding across the sky in front of me. I was glad, because the place was so strange that I wouldn't have been surprised to find the whole city had vanished.

Which goes to show you should always trust your instincts. I didn't know a thing about *Them* then, or the ways of the worlds, but I had got it right. By instinct.

What I should have done was climb back over that wall at once. I wish I had. But you know a bit what I was like by now, and I don't think *you* would have gone away either. It was so strange, this silence. And there seemed no harm in it. I knew I was scared stiff, really, but I told myself that was just the way you feel when you're trespassing. So, with my back like a mass of soft little creeping caterpillars, I went down through the trees to the mown grass at the bottom.

There was a little white statue there. Now, I'm not artistic. I saw it was of a fellow with no clothes on—I always wonder why it's Art to take your clothes off: they never put in the goose pimples—and this fellow was wrapped in chains. He didn't look as if he was enjoying himself, and small wonder. But the thing that really interested me was the way the artist had managed to carve the chains out of stone, all linked together in one piece, just as if they were real chains. I moved one to see, and it *was* just like a real chain, only made of stone. When I lifted it, I found it was fastened to the same place as all the other chains, down at one side, into the ring of what looked like a ship's anchor, and this anchor was carved half buried in the white stone the statue was standing on.

That was all I noticed, not being artistic, because by that time I could see a stone building up among the trees at the wide end of the park. I went there, very softly, hiding among the trees and bushes. My back was still creeping, but I'd got used to that by then.

When I got there, I found it was quite a big building, like a small castle, built out of pinkish gray stone. It was triangular, like the park. The part I was looking at was the pointed end. It had battlements along the top, and some quite big windows in the ground floor. You could see it had been modernized. I slithered round until I could look in one of the big windows. I couldn't get close, because there was a neat gravel terrace running round it under the windows. So what I did see was sort of smeary and dark, with the reflections of trees over it. I thought that was because I was ten feet away. I know better now.

I saw a fellow inside who seemed to be wearing a sort of cloak. Anyway, it was long and grayish and flowing, and it had a hood. The hood was not up. It was bunched back round his neck, but even so I couldn't see much of his face. You never do see *Their* faces. I thought it was just the reflections in the window then, and I craned forward to see. He was leaning over a sort of slope covered with winking lights and buttons. I knew it was a machine of some sort. I might have been ignorant, but I had climbed up into the signal box on the railway under the canal arch, and I had been shown the printing press in the court up the street, so I knew it must be a kind of machine I didn't know, but a bit like both and a lot smoother-looking. As I looked, the fellow put out a hand and very firmly and deliberately punched several buttons on the machine. Then he turned and seemed to say something across his bunched hood. Another fellow in the same sort of cloak came into sight. *They* stood with *Their* backs to me, watching something on the machine. Watching like anything. There was a terrible intentness to the way *They* stood.

It made me hold my breath. I nearly burst before one of *Them* nodded, then the other. *They* moved off then, in a cheerful busy way, to somewhere out of sight of the window. I wished I could see. I knew *They* were going to do something important. But I never saw. I only felt. The ground suddenly trembled, and the trees, and the triangular castle. They sort of shook, the way hot air does. I trembled too, and felt a peculiar twitch, as if I'd been pulled to one side all over. Then the feeling stopped. Nothing more happened.

After a moment, I crept away, until I came to the wall round the park. I was scared—yes—but I was furiously interested too. I kept wondering what made that twitch, and why everything had trembled.

As soon as I was over the wall again, it was as if my ears had popped. I could hear trains clanking and traffic rumbling—almost a roar of city noise—and that made me more interested than ever. I dropped down into the side street beyond the wall and went along to the busy street where the front of the castle was. On this side the castle was blacker-looking and guarded from the pavement by an iron paling like a row of harpoons. Behind the railings, the windows were all shuttered, in dark steel shutters. The upper windows were just slits, but they had harpoons across them too.

I looked up and I thought, No way to get in here. Yes, I was thinking of getting in from the moment I felt that twitch. I had to know what strange silent thing was going on inside. I went along the railings to the front door. It was shut, and black, and not very big. But I could tell, somehow, that it was massively heavy. There was an engraved plate screwed to the middle of the door. I didn't dare go up the four steps to the door, but I could see the plate quite well from the pavement. It was done in gold, on black, and it said:

THE OLD FORT
MASTERS OF THE REAL AND ANCIENT GAME

And underneath was the stamped-out shape of a ship's anchor. That was all. It had me almost dancing with interest and frustration.

I had to go home then, or my mother would have known I was out. She never did like me to hang around in the streets. Of course I couldn't tell her where I'd been, but I was so curious that I did ask a few casual questions.

"I was reading a book today," I said to her. "And there was something in it I didn't know. What's Masters of the Real and Ancient Game?"

"Sounds like deer hunting to me," my mother said, pouring out the tea. "Take this cup through to your father in the shop."

I took the tea through and asked my father. He had a different theory. "Sounds like one of those secret societies," he said. My hair began to prickle and try to stand up. "You know—silly stuff," my father said. "Grown men swearing oaths and acting daft mumbo-jumbo."

"This one's at the Old Fort," I said.

"Where's that?" said my father. "Never heard of it."

Mumbo-jumbo, I thought. Well, those cloaks were that all right, but it doesn't explain the machines and the twitch. Next morning, for a wonder, I went straight to school and asked my teacher before lessons. He didn't know either. I could tell he didn't, because he gave me a long talk, until the bell went, all about how *real* meant *royal* and that could apply both to tennis and to deer hunting, and how the old kings kept whole lumps of country to themselves to hunt deer in, and then on about Freemasons, in case that was what it meant. When the bell went, I asked him quickly about the Old Fort. And he had never heard of it, but he told me to go and ask at the Public Library, if I was interested.

I went to the Library on the way home from

school. The Librarian there might have been my teacher's twin. He wore the same sort of beard and half-moon spectacles and went on and on in the same way. And he didn't know either. He gave me a book on chess and another on tennis and another on hunting—none of them the slightest use—and one called *Buildings of Note*. That was not much use either. It actually had a picture of the Old Fort, one of those beautifully neat gray drawings of the front of it, harpoons and all. Underneath that, someone had spilt ink all over what it said.

I was so annoyed that, like a fool, I took it and showed it to the Librarian. And he thought I'd done it. That's the worst of being a boy. You get blamed foreverything. I still haven't got used to it. He howled and he raved and he ordered me out. And I had to go. It made me more determined than ever to find out about the Old Fort. I was so annoyed.

That ink was no accident. I thought that even then. There was no ink anywhere else on the book. *They* don't want people to know. It would have looked odd if there had been nothing about the Old Fort. Someone would have tried to find out. So *They* let it get into the book and then made sure no one could read it. That's the way *They* do things.

"You think you've put me off, don't you?" I said to *Them* in the street outside the Library. "Well, you're wrong."

I went home. It was order day. In the shop, my father was packing piles of groceries in cardboard boxes to take round to customers. Rob usually took them. As I told you, Rob liked all things to do with the shop. But I was there, so I was roped in too. For once, that was just what I wanted. Rob was annoyed. He was afraid I was going to want to ride the tricycle. Rob loved that thing, and so did my father—I can't think why. It weighed about a ton, and it had a solid metal box in front to put the cardboard boxes in. Once you had even one box of groceries aboard, your legs creaked just getting the trike moving, and the only way you could go was either in a straight line forward, or round in a tight circle. I let Rob have it. I took up the nearest box and carried it off. As soon as I was out of sight of Rob, I threw away the note on top which said *Mrs. Macready* and carried the box, groceries and all, down to the Old Fort.

Not a bad idea, I thought, as I went up the steps to the thick shut front door. I rang at the brass bell beside it and heard it go *clang clang clang* in the silence deep inside. My heart seemed to be clanging too, so hard that it hurt. Then I waited. When one of *Them* came, I was going to say, "Your groceries, sir. Like me to put them in the kitchen for you?" Not a bad idea.

I waited. And I waited. The stamped-out anchor was on the part of the door plate level with my eyes, and now, while I waited, I stared at it and saw that there was a crown over the end of it—the part they call the shank. And, after a while, my heart stopped clanging and I began to get annoyed. I rang again. And a third time. By that time I was hating that crowned anchor personally—but nothing like I did later. I've come upon pubs and inns all over the place called The Crown and Anchor. No matter how desperate I am, I can't ever bring myself to go into them. I always suspect that *They* are waiting inside.

Around five o'clock, I saw that it was no good. This is ridiculous! I thought. What do they do for groceries? Don't they eat? But really what I thought was that five o'clock was after office hours, and that the fellows had probably taken off their gray cloaks and gone home.

Well, there was an easy answer to that one. Go and take a look. What a fool I was!

So round the corner to the side street goes this fool, carrying his box of groceries, along to the best place to climb the wall. I put the box down in the street and used it to tread on to get a leg up. There was an awful squishy crunching as I took off from it—eggs probably—but I took no notice and got on top of the wall. Maybe I was more scared than I would admit. I did stay on top of that wall a minute or so. I discovered that if I put my head right over, the noise from the city went, just like that. Then if I moved my head back again—pop!—the noises were back. I did that several times before I finally swung down into the silence among the trees. Then furious curiosity took hold again. I refused to be beat. I crept to the place where I could look in that window again.

And *They* were there. Both of *Them*, lounging in a sort of chatty way beside *Their* machine, half hidden from me by the milky reflections of trees.

That settled it. *They* must have heard the bell and hadn't bothered to answer. Obviously it was very secret, what *They* did. So it stood to reason that it was worth finding out about. It also stood to reason that this park, or garden, where I was, was *Their* private one, and *They* must come out and walk in it from time to time. Which meant there had to be a door round on the other wall of the triangular fort, the wall I hadn't seen.

I went round there, through the bushes. And, sure enough, there was a door, in the middle of that side. A much more easy and approachable-looking door than that front door. It was made of flat glass, with a handle in the glass. I looked carefully, but it seemed dark behind the glass. All I could see were the reflections of the park in it and the reflection of the canal too. Its arches were right above me on that side. But what I didn't see was my own reflection in that door as I dashed across the gravel. I should have thought about that. But I didn't. It was probably too late by then anyway.

The door opened on to a sort of humming vagueness. I was inside before I knew it. *They* both turned round to look at me. Of course I saw what a fool I'd been then. The building was triangular. There was no room for the door to open anywhere except into the room with the machines. I had assumed that it didn't, because I hadn't been able to see it through the glass door. There were the machines in front of me now, a triangular patch of them, winking and blinking, and I ought to have been able to see them just as clearly through that door.

An awful lot in that place was vague, including *Them*. The shadow of the canal was in here too, and the only things I could see clearly were those that happened to come in the slabs of dark shadow where the arches were. In between, it was white sky, with everything confused in it. *They* were in the sky. You never see *Them* clearly. All I did see was a huge table standing down at the wide end of the triangular room. There was a sort of flickering going on over it and some huge regular shapes hanging in the air above it. I blinked at those shapes. They were like enormous dice.

So there *is* a game going on! I thought.

But it was the queerest feeling. It was like having got into a reflection in a shop window. And, at the same time, I had a notion I was really standing outside in the open air, under the canal arches somewhere. I thought at first that it was this feeling that kept me standing there. I thought I was plain confused. It only came to me gradually that I was sort of hanging there, and that I couldn't move at all.

II

The one of *Them* nearest me walked round behind
me and shut the door. "Another random factor," he
said. He sounded annoyed. It was the way my
mother would say, "Bother! We've got mice again."

And the other one said, "We'd better deal with
that before we go on then." He said it the way my
father would answer, "You'd better set traps again,
my dear."

"How?" asked the first one, coming back round
me to the machines. "Can we afford a corpse at this
stage? I do wish we could do without these
randoms."

"Oh but we can't," said the other. "We need
them. Besides, the risk adds to the fun. I think we'd
better discard this one to the Bounder circuits—but
let's get a readout first on the effect of a corpse on
play."

"Right you are," said the first one.

They both leaned over the machines. I could see
Them through the white sheets of reflected sky,
looking at me carefully and then looking down to

press another button. It was the way my mother kept looking at the color of our curtains when she was choosing new wallpaper. After that, *They* turned their attention to another part of the machine and gazed at it, rather dubiously. Then *They* went down the room to look at that huge flickering table.

"Hm," said the first one. "Play is quite delicately poised at the moment, isn't it?"

"Yes," said the second. "If it was on your side, it would help bring your revolution closer, but I can't afford any urban unrest for a couple of decades or more. I claim unfair hazard. Let's discard. Agreed?"

The first one came back and stood looking into the machine in the intent way *They* did. "It would make good sense," he said, "if we could go back over the family of this discard and scrub all memory of it."

"Oh no," said the other, moving up too. "It's against the rules for a discard. The anchor, you know. The anchor."

"But we can scrub with a corpse. Why don't we?"

"Because I've already claimed unfair hazard. Come on. Make it a discard."

"Yes, why not?" said the first one. "It's not that important. What's the rule? These days we have to check with the rest in case the Bounder circuits are overloaded, don't we?"

As I sit here, it's true! *They* said all that, talking about me just as if I were a wooden counter or a piece of card in a game. And I floated there and couldn't do a thing about it. Next thing I knew, *They* were punching more buttons, round the end of the machines.

And the place opened up.

You know if you go to a barber's shop with a lot of mirrors, how you can sit looking into one mirror and see through it into the mirror behind you, over and over again, until it goes all blurred with distance? Well, what happened was like that. Over and over again, and all blurred, there were suddenly triangular rooms all round. They were slotted in on both sides, and beyond and behind that, and underneath, down and down. They were piled up on top of us too. I looked, but it made me feel ill, seeing two of *Them* walking about up there, and others of *Them* above and beside that, all strolling over where *They* could see me. *They* all wore those cloaks, but *They* weren't just reflections of the first two. *They* were all different from one another. That was about all I could tell. It was all so blurry and flickery, and the reflection of the canal arches went striding through the lot, as if that was the only real thing there.

"Your attention for a moment," said one of *Them* who was with me. "We are about to make a discard. Can you confirm that there is still room on the Bounds?"

A distant voice said, "Computing."

A nearer, hollower voice asked, "What's the reason for the discard?"

The second one of my *Them* said, "We've had an

intrusion by a random factor, entailing the usual danger of feedback into the native world here. I've claimed unfair hazard against reinsertion as a corpse."

"That seems adequate," said the hollow voice.

Almost at once, the distant voice said, "The Bounds have space for four more discards. Repeat, four more only. Is the reason good enough?"

There was a little murmuring. For a moment, I thought I was going to end up as a corpse. I still didn't know what I was in for, you see. Then the murmur grew—with an air of surprise to it, as if *They* were wondering what *They* were being asked for. "Reason sufficient. Sufficient reason," came rumbling from all round, above and underneath.

"Then I must caution you," said the hollow voice. "Rule seventy-two thousand now comes into play. The final three discards must only be made with extreme caution and at the most pressing need."

With that, *They* all faded away, into the reflection of the sky again, and left just my two.

The second one came sweeping towards me. The first was standing with his hand ready on a handle of some kind. The second one spoke to me, slowly and carefully, as if I was an idiot. "You are now a discard," he said. "We have no further use for you in play. You are free to walk the Bounds as you please, but it will be against the rules for you to enter play in any world. To ensure you keep this rule, you will be transferred to another field of play every time a move ends in the field where you are. The rules also state that you are allowed to return Home if you can. If you succeed in returning Home, then you may enter play again in the normal manner."

I looked up at him. He was a gray blurred figure behind a sheet of white reflected sky. So was the other one, and he was just about to pull down the lever. "Hey! Wait a minute!" I said. "What's all this? What are these rules? Who made them?"

Both of *Them* stared at me. *They* looked like you would if your breakfast egg had suddenly piped up and said, "Don't eat me!"

"You've no right to send me off without any explanation, like this!" I said.

He pulled the lever while I was saying it. You might whack your egg on top with your spoon the same way. The sideways twitch came while I was saying "explanation." As I said "like this!" I was somewhere else entirely.

And I mean somewhere else. It's hard to explain just how different it was. I was standing out in the open, just as I'd half thought that I was out in the open under the canal arches before, only this was real, solid and real. There was green grass going up and down over hills in all directions. Across the valley in front of me, there was a group of black-and-white animals, eating the grass. I thought they were cows, probably. I'd never seen a live cow till then. Beyond that, going up against the sunset, was a spire of smoke. And that was all. The place was empty otherwise, except for me. I turned right round to make sure, and it was the truth.

That was shock enough, if you were a city boy like me. It was a horrible feeling. I wanted to crouch down and get my eyes to the top of my head somehow, like a frog, so that I could see all round me at once. But there was more to it than that. The air in that place was soft and mild. It smelled different and it felt different. It weighed on you in a different way, sort of sluggishly. The grass didn't look quite right, and even the sun, setting down over the hill where the spire of smoke was, was not like the sun I was used to. It was making the sunset the wrong color.

While I was turning round the second time, it came to me that the slanting dip in the valley just behind me was the same shape as *Their* triangular park, where the statue was. Then I looked very carefully over the rest of the green slopes. Yes. The valley in front was where the smart part of the city should be, and the railway, and the hill beside me, and the one where the sun was setting, were the two hills the canal went between on its arches. The slope on the other side of me was going up to where our courtyard should have been. But the city had gone.

"I hate *Them*!" I screamed out. Because I knew then, without having to think it out, that I was on another world. This world seemed to have the same shape as mine, but it was different in every other way. And I didn't know how to get back to mine.

For a while, I stood there and yelled every cussword I knew at *Them*, and I knew quite a few, even then. Then I set off to walk to that line of smoke going up into the sunset. There must be a house there, I thought. There's no point starving. And, as I walked, I thought over very carefully what *They* had said. *They* had talked of Bounds and Bounder circuits and discards and random factors and rules. I could see those were words in an enormous serious game. And I was a random factor, so *They* had discarded me, but there were still rules for that. And these rules said—The one who spoke to me at the end might have talked as if I was an idiot, but the way he had done it was rather like a policeman talks to someone he's arresting: "Everything you say can be taken down and may be used in evidence." *They* had told me the rules, and those said I could get Home if I could manage it. Well I would. I might be a discard on the Bounder circuits, but I was a Homeward Bounder, and *They* had better not forget it! I was going to get Home and spite *Them*. Then *They* had better watch out!

By this time, I had got near the cows. Cows are always bigger than you expect, and their horns are sharp. They have this upsetting way of stopping eating when you come up, and staring. I stopped and stared back. I was scared. I didn't even dare turn round and go back, in case they came galloping up behind me and pronged me on those horns like toast on a toasting fork. Heaven knows what I would have done, if some men had not come galloping up just then to round up the cows. They were hairy, dirty men, dressed in cowhide, and their horses were as bad. They all stared at me, men, horses and cows, and one of those men was the image of the printer who owned the printing press in the courtyard up the road from ours.

That made me feel much better. I didn't think he *was* the printer—and he wasn't of course—but I got on with the printer, and I thought I could get on with this copy of him too. "Hello," I said. "You don't happen to want a boy for odd jobs, do you?"

He grinned, a big hairy split in his beard. And he answered. And here was another blow. It was gabble. I could not understand one word. They spoke quite a different language to mine.

"Oh mother!" I wailed. "I'll get *Them* for this, if it's the last thing I do!"

In fact, the hairy herdsmen were nice to me. I was lucky in a way. Some Homeward Bounders have to begin much harder than I did. Allowing for language problems, my start wasn't at all bad. They helped me up on the horse behind the printer, and they rode off with me and the cows to where they lived. And they lived in tents—a set of large smelly leather tents with the hair still on them in patches. The line of smoke was from the sort of bonfire they used for cooking on. I felt I could stand that. I told myself it was an adventure. But I couldn't stand their Chief. She was a great huge wobbly woman with a voice like a train whistle. She was always scolding. She scolded the men for bringing me and me for coming, and me for speaking gibberish and wearing peculiar clothes, and the fire for burning and the sun for setting. Or I think she did. It took me days to understand the first word of their lingo.

I've got used to learning languages since. You get a system. But this one was a real shocker anyhow—they had sixteen words for *cow* and if you got the wrong one, they fell about laughing—and I think I wasn't trying properly. I wasn't expecting to be there that long. I was going Home. And it didn't help that Mrs. Chief decided to give me language lessons herself. She had the idea that if she scolded loud enough I would have to understand by sheer noise-power. We used to sit cross-legged facing one another, her scolding away at top shriek, and me nodding and smiling.

"That's right," I would say, nodding intelligently. "Yell away, you old squish-bag."

At this, she would be pleased, because I seemed to be trying, and scream louder than ever. And I would smile.

"And you smell too," I would say. "Worse than any of your cows."

Well, it kept me sane. And it gave her an interest in life. It was pretty boring, life on the cattle-range. The only excitement they had was if a bull got nasty, or another tribe of herders went by on the horizon. All the same, I had to keep telling myself very firmly,

"This is not so bad. It could be worse. It's not a bad life." That kept me sane too.

After six weeks or so, I had the hang of the language. I could sit on a horse without finding myself sitting on the ground the next second, and I could help round up cows. I was learning how to make leather rope and tan leather and weave hurdles, and a dozen other useful things. But I never learned how to milk a cow. That was sacred. Only women were allowed to do that. And at this stage, they took down their tents and moved on to find better grass. They never reckoned to stay in one place much over a month.

I was riding along with them, helping keep the cattle together, when, about midday, I had the most peculiar sensation. It was like being pulled, strongly and remorselessly, sideways from the way we were going. With it, came a worse feeling—from inside me. It was a terrible yearning and a longing. My throat hurt with it. And it was like an itch too. I wanted to get inside my head and scratch. Both feelings were so strong that I had to turn my horse the way they pulled me, and as soon as I had, I felt better—as if I was now doing the right thing. And, no sooner was I trotting away in that direction, than I was full of excitement. I was going Home. I was sure of it. This was how you were moved along the Bounds. I had been right to think I was only going to be a short time in this world.

(That was about the only thing I was right

about, as it happened. You nearly always get a feeling, when you first come into a world, how long you're going to have to stay there. I've only ever known myself wrong once. And that time was twice as long as I thought. I think one of *Them* must have changed his mind about his move.)

On this first occasion, Mrs. Chief sent two hairy riders after me and they rounded me up just like a cow.

"What do you think you're doing, going off on your own like that?" she screamed at me. "Suppose you meet an enemy!"

"First I heard you *had* any enemies," I said sulkily. The pulling and the yearning were terrible.

She made me ride in the middle of the girls after that, and wouldn't listen to anything I said. I've learned to hold my tongue when the Bounds call now. It saves trouble. Then, I had to wait till night came, and it was agony. I felt pulled out of shape by the pull and sick with the longing—really sick: I couldn't eat supper. Waste of a good beef steak. Worse still, I was all along haunted by the idea I was going to be too late. I was going to miss my chance of getting Home. I had to get to some particular place in order to move to other worlds, and I wasn't going to get there in time.

It was quite dark when at last I got the chance to slip away. It was a bit cloudy and there was no moon—some worlds don't have moons: others have anything up to three—but that didn't matter to me.

The Bounds called so strongly that I knew exactly which way to head. I went that way at a run. I ran all through the warm moisty night. I was drowned in sweat and panting like someone sawing wood. In the end, I was falling down every few yards, getting up again, and staggering on. I was so scared I'd be too late. By the time the sun rose, I think I was simply going from one foot to the other, almost on the spot. Stupid. I've learned better since. But this was the first time, and, when there was light, I shouted out with joy. There was a green flat space among the green hills ahead, and someone had marked the space with a circle of wooden posts.

At that, I managed to trot and lumbered into the circle. Somewhere near the middle of it, the twitch took me sideways again.

You've probably guessed what happened. You can imagine how I felt anyway. It was dawn still, a lurid streaky dawn. The green ranges had gone, but there was no city—nothing like one. The bare lumpy landscape round me was heaped with what looked like piles of cinders, and each pile had its own dreary little hut standing beside it. I had no idea what they were—they were mines, actually. You weren't a person in that new world if you didn't have your own hole and keep digging coal or copper out of it. But I didn't care what was going on. I was feeling the air, as I did before, and realizing that this was yet another different world. And at the same time, I realized that I was due to stay here for rather a long time.

It was on this world that I began to understand that *They* hadn't told me even half the rules. *They* had just told me the ones that interested *Them*. On this world I was starved and hit, and buried under a collapsed slag-heap. I'm not going to describe it. I hate it too much. I was there twice too, because what happened was that I got caught in a little ring of worlds and went all round the ring two times. At the time, I thought they were all the worlds there were — except for Home, which I never seemed to get to — and I thought of them as worlds, which they are not, not really.

They are separate universes, stacked in together like I saw the triangular rooms of *Them* before *They* sent me off. These universes all touch somewhere — and where they touch is the Boundary — but they don't mix. Homeward Bounders seem to be the only people who can go from one universe to another. And we go by walking the Bounds until we come to a Boundary, when, if one of *Them* has finished his move, we get twitched into the Boundary in another Earth, in another universe. I only understood this properly when I got to the sixth world round, where the stars are all different.

I looked at those stars. "Jamie boy," I said. "This is crazy." Possibly I was a little crazy then, too, because Jamie answered me, and said, "They're probably the stars in the Southern hemisphere — Australia and all that." And I answered him. "It's still crazy," I said. "This world's upside down then."

It was upside down, in more ways than that. The
Them that played it must have been right peculiar.
But it was that which made me feel how separate
and—well—*universal* each world was. And how
thoroughly I was a discard, a reject, wandering
through them all and being made to move on all the
time. For a while after that, I went round seeing all
worlds as nothing more than colored lights on a
wheel reflected on a wall. *They* are turning the wheel
and lighting the lights, and all we get is the
reflections, no more real than that. I still see it that
way sometimes. But when you get into a new world,
it's as solid as grass and granite can make it, and the
sky shuts you in just as if there was no way through.
Then you nerve yourself up. Here comes the grind of
finding out its ways and learning its language.

You wouldn't believe how lonely you get.

But I was going to tell you about the rules that
They didn't tell me. I mentioned some of the trouble
I had in the mining world. I had more in other
worlds. And none of these things killed me. Some of
them ought to have done, specially that slag-heap—
I was under it for days. And that is the rule: call it
Rule One. A random factor like me, walking the
Bounds, has to go on. Nothing is allowed to stop
him. He can starve, fall off a mile-high temple, get
buried, and still he goes on. The only way he can
stop is to come Home.

People can't interfere with a Homeward Bounder

either. That may be part of Rule One, but I prefer to call it Rule Two. If you don't believe people can't interfere with me, find me and try it. You'll soon see: I'll tell you—on my fifth world, I had a little money for once. A whole gold piece, to be precise. I got an honest job in a tannery—and carried the smell right through to the next world with me too. On my day off, I was strolling in the market looking for my favorite cakes. They were a little like Christmas puddings with icing on—gorgeous! Next thing I knew, a boy about my own age had come up beside me, given me a chop-and, chop-and—it darned well hurt too—and run off with my gold piece. Naturally, I yelled and started to run after him. But he was under a wagon the next moment, dead as our neighbor's little girl back Home. His hand with the gold piece in it was sticking out, just as if he was handing it back to me, but I hadn't the heart to take it. I couldn't. It felt like my fault, that wagon.

After a while, I told myself I was imagining that rule. That boy's corpse could have had a bad effect on play, just as *They* said mine would have done. But I think that was one of the things *They* meant by the risk adding to the fun. I didn't imagine that rule. The same sort of thing happened to me several times later on. The only one I didn't feel bad about was a rotten Judge who was going to put me in prison for not being able to bribe him. The roof of the courthouse fell in on him.

Rule Three isn't too good either. Time doesn't

act the same in any world. It sort of jerks about as you go from one to another. But time hardly acts at all on a Homeward Bounder. I began to see that rule on my second time round the circle of worlds. The second time I got to the upside down one, for instance, nearly ten years had gone by, but only eight or so when I got to the next one. I still don't know how much of my own time I spent going round that lot, but I swear I was only a few days older. It seemed to me I had to be keeping the time of my own Home. But, as I told you, I still only seem about thirteen years old, and I've been on a hundred worlds since then.

By the time I had all this worked out, I was well on my second round of the circle. I had learned I wasn't going to get Home anything like as easily as I had thought. Sometimes I wondered if I was ever going to get there. I went round with an ache like a cold foot inside me over it. Nothing would warm that ache. I tried to warm it by remembering Home, and our courtyard and my family, in the tiniest detail. I remembered things I had not really noticed when they happened—silly things, like how particular our mother was over our boots. Boots cost a lot. Some of the kids in the court went without in summer, and couldn't play football properly, but we never went without. If my mother had to cut up her old skirt to make Elsie a dress in order to afford them, we never went without boots. And I used to take that for granted. I've gone barefoot enough since, I can tell you.

And I remembered even the face Elsie used to make—she sort of pushed her nose down her face so that she looked like a camel—when Rob's old boots were mended for her to wear. She never grumbled. She just made that face. I remember my father made a bit the same face when my mother wanted me to stay on at school. I swore to myself that I'd help him out in the shop when I did get Home. Or go grinding on at school, if that was what they decided. I'd do anything. Besides, after grinding away learning languages the way I'd done, school might almost seem lively.

I think remembering that way made the cold foot ache inside me worse, but I couldn't stop. It made me hate *Them* worse too, but I didn't mind that.

All this while, I'd never met a single other Homeward Bounder. I thought that was a rule too, that we weren't supposed to. I reckoned that we were probably set off at regular intervals, so that we never overtook one another. I knew there were others, of course. After a bit, I learned to pick up traces of them. We left signs for one another—like tramps and robbers do in some worlds—mostly at Boundaries.

It took me a long while to work the signs out, on my own. For one thing, the Boundaries varied so much, that I didn't even notice the signs until I'd learned to look for them. The ring of posts in the cattle-range world matched with a clump of trees in the fourth world, and with a dirty great temple in the seventh. In the mining world, there was nothing to mark the Boundary at all. Typical, that. I used to think that *They* had marked the Boundaries with these things, and I got out of them quick at first, until I noticed the sign carved on one of the trees. Somehow that made me feel that the people on the worlds must have marked the Boundaries. There was the same sign carved in the temple too. This sign meant GOOD PICKINGS. I earned good money in both worlds.

Then, by the time I was going round the whole collection another time, I was beginning to get the hang of the Bounds too, as well as the signs and the Boundaries. Bounds led into the Boundary from three different directions, so you could come up by another route and still go through the Boundary, but from another side. I saw more signs that way. But a funny thing was that the ordinary people in the worlds seemed to know the Bounds were there, as well as the Boundaries. They never walked the Bounds of course—they never felt the call—but they must have felt *something*. In some worlds there were towns and villages all along a Bound. In the seventh world, they thought the Bounds were sacred. I came out of the Boundary temple to see a whole line of temples stretching away into the distance, just like my cousin Marie's wedding cake, one tall white wedding cake to every hilltop.

Anyway, I was going to say there were other signs on the other two sides of the Boundaries when

I came to look. I picked up a good many that way. Then came one I'd never seen before. I've seen it quite a lot since. It means RANDOM and I'm usually glad to see it. That was how I got out of that wretched ring of worlds and met a few other Homeward Bounders at last.

III

I had got back to the cattle world by then. As soon as I arrived, I knew I was not going to be there long, and I would have been pleased, only by then I knew that the mining world came next.

"Oh please!" I prayed out loud, but not to *Them*. "Please not that blistering-oath mining world again! Anywhere else, but not that!"

The cattle country was bad enough. I never met the same people twice in it, of course. The earlier ones had moved off or died by the time I came round again. The ones I met were always agreeable, but they never *did* anything. It was the most boring place. I used to wonder if the *Them* playing it had gone to sleep on the job. Or maybe they were busy in a part of that world I never got to, and kept this bit just marking time. However it was, I was in for another session of dairy-farming, and I was almost glad it would only be a little one. Glad, that is, but for the mining horror that came next.

It was only three days before I felt the Bounds call. I was surprised. I hadn't known it would be *that*

short. By that time I had gone quite a long way down
south with a moving tribe I fell in with. They were
going down to the sea, and I wanted to go too. I had
still never seen the sea then, believe it or not. I was
really annoyed to feel the tugging, and the yearning
in my throat, start so soon.

But I was an old hand by then. I thought I would
bear it, stick it out for as long as possible, and put off
the mining world for as long as I could. So I ground
my teeth together and kept sitting on the horse
they'd lent me and jogging away south.

And suddenly the dragging and the yearning
took hold of me from a different direction, almost
from the way we were going. I was so confused I fell
off the horse. While I was sitting on the grass with
my hands over my head, waiting for the rest of the
tribe to get by before I dared get up—you get kicked
in the head if you try crawling about under a crowd
of horses—the next part of the call started: the
"Hurry, hurry, you'll be late!" It's always sooner and
stronger if you get it from a new direction. It's
always stronger from a RANDOM Boundary too. I
don't know why. This was so strong that I found I
couldn't wait any longer. I got up and started
running.

They shouted after me of course. They're scared
of people going off on their own, even though
nothing ever happens to them. But I took no notice
and kept running, and they didn't have a Mrs. Chief
with them—theirs was a sleepy girl who never

bothered about anything—so they didn't follow me. I stopped running when I was over the nearest hill and walked. I knew by then that the "Hurry, hurry!" was only meant to get me going. It didn't mean much.

It was just as well it didn't mean much. It took me the rest of that day and all night to get there, and the funny colored sun was two hours up before I saw the Boundary. This was a new one. It was marked by a ring of stones.

I stared at it a little as I went down into the valley where it was. They were such big stones. I couldn't imagine any hairy cattle herders having the energy to make it. Unless *They* had done it, of course. I stared again when I saw the new sign scrawled on the nearest huge stone, some way above my head.

"I wonder what that means," I said. But I had been a long time on the way and the call was getting almost too strong to bear. I stopped wondering and went into the circle.

And—twitch—I was drowning in an ocean.

Yes, I saw the sea after all—from inside. At least, I was inside for what seemed about five minutes, until I came screaming and drowning and kicking up to the surface, and coughing out streams of fierce salt water—only to have all my coughing undone the next moment by a huge great wave, which came and hit me *slap* in the face, and sent me under again. I came up again pretty fast. I didn't care that nothing could stop a Homeward Bounder.

I didn't believe it. I was drowning.

It isn't true what they say about your life passing before you. You're too busy. You're at it full time, bashing at the water with your arms and screaming "Help!" to nothing and nobody. And too busy keeping afloat. I hadn't the least idea how to swim. What I did was a sort of crazy jumping up and down, standing in the water, with miles more water down underneath me, bending and stretching like a mad frog, and it kept me up. It also turned me round in a circle. Every way was water, with sky at the end of it. Nothing in sight at all, except flaring sunlit water on one side and heaving gray water on the other.

That had me really panicked. I jumped and screamed like a madman. And here was a funny thing—somebody seemed to be answering. Next moment, a sort of black cliff came sliding past me, and someone definitely shouted. Something that looked like a frayed rope splashed down in the sea in front of me. I dived on it with both hands, which sent me under again, even though I caught the rope. I was hauled up like that, yelling and sousing and shivering, and went bumping up the side of that sudden black cliff.

It was like going up the side of a cheese-grater— all barnacles. I left quite a lot of skin on there, and a bit more being dragged over the top. I remember realizing it was a boat and then looking at who'd rescued me. And I think I passed out. Certainly I remember nothing else until I was lying on a mildewy bed, under a damp blanket, and thinking, This can't be true! I can't have been pulled out of the sea by a bunch of monkeys! But that was what I seemed to have seen. I knew that, even with my eyes closed. I had seen skinny thin hairy arms and shaggy faces with bright monkey eyes, all jabbering at me. It must be true, I thought. I must be in a world run by monkeys now.

At that point, someone seized my head and tried to suffocate me by pouring hellfire into my mouth. I did a lot more coughing. Then I gently opened one watery eye and took a look at the monkey who was doing it to me.

This one was a man. That was some comfort, even though he was such a queer-looking fellow. He had the remains of quite a large square face. I could see that, though a lot of it was covered by an immense black beard. Above the beard, his cheeks were so hollow that it looked as if he were sucking them in, and his eyes had gone right back into his head somehow, so that his eyebrows turned corners on top of them. His hair was as bad as his beard, like a rook's nest. The rest of him looked more normal, because he was covered up to the chin in a huge navy-blue coat with patches of mold on it. But it probably only looked normal. The hand he stretched out—with a bottle in it to choke me with hellfire again—was like a skeleton's.

I jumped back from that bottle. "No thanks. I'm fine now."

He bared his teeth at me. He was smiling. "Ah, ve can onderstand von anodder!" That is a rough idea of the way he spoke. Now, I've been all over the place, and changed my accent a good twenty times, but I always speak English like a native. He didn't. But at least I seemed to be in a world where someone spoke it.

"Who are you?" I said.

He looked reproachful at that. I shouldn't have asked straight out. "Ve ollways," he said—I can't do the way he spoke—"we always keep one sharp lookout coming through the Boundaries, in case any other Homeward Bounder in the water lies. Lucky for you, eh!"

I stared at his huge hollow face. "Are *you* one? Do you call us Homeward Bounders too?"

"That is the name to all of us is given," he said to me sadly.

"Oh," I said. "I thought I'd made it up. How long have you been one?" A long time, by the look of him, I thought.

He sighed. "You have not heard of me in your world maybe? In many places I am known, always by my ship, always sailing on. The name most often given is that of Flying Dutchman."

As it happens, I had heard of him. At school—good old boring chapel-shaped Churt House—one rainy afternoon, when all the other Dominies were down with flu. The one Dominie left had told us about the Flying Dutchman, among other stories.

But all I could remember about him was that long, long ago he had been doomed to sail on forever, until, unless—It didn't matter. It was probably the same as me.

"What happened? What did you do to annoy *Them*?" I asked.

He shivered, and sort of put me aside with that skeleton hand of his. "It is not permitted to speak of these things," he said. Then he seemed sorry. "But you are only young. You will learn."

"What world do you come from, then?" I asked. "Is it permitted to speak of that? Is it the same world as me?" I sat up then, in great excitement, thinking that if we were both from the same place, then we were Bound to the same Home, and I could do worse than sail with him until we got there. Sitting up gave me a view of the cabin. I was not so sure after that. Cobwebs hung in swags from all the corners and beams. On the walls, black mold and green slime were fighting it out to see which could climb highest, and every piece of metal I could see was rusty, including the candlestick on the wormy table. The cabin floor had dirty water washing about on it, this way and that as the boat swung, and swilling round the Dutchman's great seaboots. "Is yours the same world?" I said doubtfully.

"I do not know," he said sadly. "But I shall know if I am back there. There will be some rest then."

"Well, I'll tell you about my Home," I said. "You may recognize something. First, my name's Jamie H—"

But he raised his skeleton hand again. "Please. We do not give names. We think it is not permitted."

Here, one of his crew came to the door and did a jabber-jabber. He was a man too, but I saw why I had taken him for a monkey. He was so stick-thin. He was more or less naked too, and the parts of him that weren't burnt dark brown were covered with hair. Men are very like monkeys really.

The Dutchman listened for a little. Then he said, "Ja, ja," and got up and went out.

It was not very interesting in the cabin and it smelled of mold, so after a bit I got up and went on deck too. The sea was there, all round. It gave me the pip at first, just like the wide-open cattle country. But you get used to it quite soon. The sailors were all scrambling about the rakish masts above me. They were struggling with the great black torn sails, and they seemed to be trying to hoist a few more. Every so often, a rotten rope would snap. There would be some resigned jabber, and they would mend it and carry on. This made it quite a long business, getting any extra sails up.

The Dutchman was standing with his hands in his pockets, watching the reason for all this pother. It was another ship, a beauty, about midway between us and the horizon. It was like an arrow or a bird, that ship—like everything quick and beautiful. I had to gasp when I saw it. It had a bank of white sails, white as a swan. But, as I watched, I could see frenzied activity among those white sails. Shortly, a whole lot more white sails came up, some above, some overlapping the others, until there were so many sails up that you thought the thing was going to topple over and sink from sheer top-heaviness. Like that, the white ship turned and, with a bit of a waggle, like a hasty lady, made her way over the horizon. Our sails were still not set.

The Dutchman sighed heavily. "Always they go. They think we are unlucky."

"Are you?" I asked, rather worried on my own account.

"Only to ourselves," he sighed. He gave out some jabbering. The monkeys up aloft gave up struggling with the sails and came down to the deck again.

After that, I was sure they would be thinking of breakfast. I hadn't eaten since lunch the day before, and I was starving. Well, I suppose a Homeward Bounder can never exactly starve, but put it this way: it never feels that way, and my stomach was rolling. But time went on, and nobody said a word about food. The monkeys lay about, or carved blocks of wood, or mended ropes. The Dutchman strode up and down. In the end, I got so desperate that I asked him right out.

He stopped striding and looked at me sadly. "Eating? That we gave up long ago. There is no need to eat. A Homeward Bounder does not die."

"I know," I said. "But it makes you feel a whole lot more comfortable. Look at you. You all look like walking skeletons."

"That is true," he admitted. "But it is hard to take on board provisions when you sail on, and ever on."

I saw the force of that. "Don't you ever fetch up on land then?" And I was suddenly terrified. Suppose I was stuck on this ship, too, forever, without any food.

"Sometimes we go to land, ja," the Dutchman admitted. "When we come through a Boundary and we can tell we have time, we find an island where is privacy, and we land. We eat then sometimes. We may eat maybe when we come to land to put you ashore."

That relieved my mind considerably. "You should eat," I said earnestly. "Do, to please me. Can't you catch fish, or something?"

He changed the subject. Perhaps he thought catching fish was not permitted. He thought no end of things were not permitted. I had opportunity to know how many things, because I was on that ship for days. And a more uncomfortable time I hope never to spend. Everything about that ship was rotten. It was half waterlogged. Water squeezed out of the boards when you trod on them and mold grew on everything. And nobody cared. That was what got me so annoyed. True, I could see they'd been at this game for ages, a hundred times longer than I had, and they had a right to be miserable. But they took it to such lengths!

"Can't you wear a few more clothes?" I said to a monkey every so often. "Where's your self-respect?"

He would just look at me and jabber. None of them spoke much English. After a bit, I began to ask it in another sort of way, because it got colder. Fog hung in the air and made the damp ship even wetter. I shivered. But the monkeys just shrugged. They were past caring.

I thought it was another piece of the same when I looked over the side of the ship on about the fourth foggy day. By then, anything would have been interesting. I noticed there were two big iron holes there, in the front, each with a length of rusty chain dangling out of them. I had seen pictures of ships. I knew what should have been there.

"Don't you even carry anchors?" I asked the Dutchman. "How do you stop?"

"No," he said. "We threw them away long ago."

I was so hungry that it made me snappish. "What a stupid thing to do!" I said. "That's you lot all over, with your stupid negative attitude! Can't you think positive for once? You wouldn't be in half this mess if you did. Fancy throwing anchors away!"

He just stood there, looking at me sadly and, I thought, sort of meaningly. And suddenly I remembered the crowned anchor on the front of the Old Fort. I knew better than to mention *Them* to him by then. He never would come straight out like I did and call them *Them*. He always put it impersonally: It is not permitted. But of course he knew that anchors had something to do with *Them*—probably better than I did. "Oh, I see," I said. "Sorry."

"We took them off," he said, "to show that we are without hope. Hope is an anchor, you know."

A bit of good came of this, though. He got worried about me, I think. He thought I was young and ignorant and hot-headed. He asked me what kind of Boundary I had come in by. "I am afraid," he said, "that you may have got on a circuit that is sea only, and next time I will not be by. I shall put you on land, because I think it is not permitted for us to stay in company, but you may still end up in the water all the same."

Oh he was a cheery fellow. But kind. I told him about the stone Boundary and the strange sign.

"That is all right," he said. "That is RANDOM. Look for the same again and you will unlikely be drowned."

It turned out that he knew no end more signs than I did. I suspect that he'd been Homeward Bound so long that he may even have invented some of them. He wrote them all out for me with a rusty nail on his cabin door. They were mostly general ones like UNFRIENDLY and GOOD CLIMATE. I gave him a few particular ones I knew in return, including one I thought would be really useful: YOU CAN NICK FOOD HERE.

"I thank you," he said solemnly.

A day later, thank goodness, we came to some land. It was not my idea of heaven. I could hardly see it in the fog, for a start, and what I could see was wet rocks and spouts of wave breaking over them. It made me feel the ship was not so bad after all.

"Maybe we should go on a bit," I said nervously to the Dutchman. "This looks rough. It could break your ship up."

He stood somberly beside me, with his navy coat and his beard and his hair all dewed with fog, watching the spouting waves come nearer through the whiteness. "The ship does not break," he said. "It does not matter. There are seven holes in the underside and still we float. We cannot stop. We go on floating and sailing forever." Then he did something I never thought to see him do. He took his fist out of his pocket and he shook it, shook it savagely in the air. "And we know why!" he shouted out. "All for a game. A *game*!"

"I bet that's not permitted," I said.

He put his hand in his pocket again. "Maybe," he said. "I do not care. You must make ready to jump when we are near enough. Do not be afraid. You cannot be hurt."

Well, we came near, and I sort of flounderingly jumped. Perhaps I couldn't be hurt, but I could be pounded and grazed and drenched and winded, and I was. I was so weak with hunger too that it took me ages to drag myself out of the surf and scramble up onto a wet lump of granite. Then I turned to wave to the Flying Dutchman. They all crowded to the side and waved back, him and the monkeys. I could hardly see them through the fog. It looked like a ghost ship out there, ragged and sketchy, like a gray pencil drawing, and it seemed to be tipping to one side rather. I suspect there were now eight holes underneath it. There had been a lot of grinding and rending while I was struggling up the rock.

It simply melted into the fog as I looked. I stood there all alone, shivering. I remembered then what my teacher had said, that rainy afternoon at Home, about the Flying Dutchman. It was supposed to be a ghost ship.

But it wasn't, I told myself. Nor was I a ghost. We were all Homeward Bound, and I for one was going to get there. I just wished I wasn't on my own. The Flying Dutchman was much better off. There was a crowd of them, to my one. They would be in clover, compared with me, if only they could have brought themselves to care about things a bit more.

After this, I set off inland, climbing, slipping and sliding, to where the strangest thing yet happened to me. It was so strange that, even if *They*'d done nothing, there would still have been times when I would have sworn it was a vision or something, brought on by lack of food. But I know it happened. It was realler than I am.

IV

I was very thirsty. It was worse than the hunger. You'd have thought with a wet ship like that, I'd have been all right, but it was all salt, apart from the fog. And the salt I'd swallowed getting on land made me thirstier than before. I don't know how the Flying Dutchman managed. The only drink they had was the firewater he had choked me with, and I think they saved that for using on people they'd fished out of the sea.

But as soon as I got high enough up the rocks and far enough inland not to hear nothing but sea, I could hear water trickling. You know that hollow pouring sound a little stream makes coming down through rocks. I heard that, and it made my mouth dry up and go thick. I was so thirsty I could have cried. I set out scrambling and slithering through the fog towards the noise.

That white wet fog confused everything. I think, if I hadn't been so thirsty, I'd never have found it. The rocks were terrible — a total jumble. They were all hard, hard pinkish granite, so hard that nothing grew on it, and so wet that I was always slithering onto my face. That hurt at least as much as scraping up the side of the Flying Dutchman's ship. You know how granite seems to be made of millions of grains, pink and black and gray and white—well, every one of those grains scratched me separately, I swear.

After a while, I had got quite high up somewhere, and the lovely hollow pouring sound was coming from quite near, over to the right. I slithered over that way and had to stop short. There was a huge split in the granite there, and a great deep hole, and I could hear the pouring coming from the other side of the split.

"Unprintable things!" I said—only I didn't say that. I really said them. But I hate to be beat. You know that by now. I went down into the hole and then climbed up the other side. I don't know how I did it. When I dragged myself out the other side, my arms felt like bits of string and wouldn't answer when I tried to bunch my fists up, and my legs were not much better. I was covered with scratches too. I must have been a sight.

The pouring was really near now, from the other side of a lump of crag. I crawled my way round it. It was a great rock sticking up at the top of the hill, and there was a ledge on the other side about eight feet wide, if that. And there I had to stop short again, because there was a man chained to the crag, between me and the water.

He looked to be dead or dying. He was sort of

collapsed back on the rock with his eyes shut. His face was tipped back from me—I was still crouching down, weak as a kitten—but I could see his face was near on as hollow as the Flying Dutchman's, and it looked worse, because this man hadn't a beard, only reddish stubble. His hair was reddish too, but it was soaking wet with him being out in the fog and the rain like this, and you could hardly tell it from the granite. His clothes, such as there was left of them, were soaking too, of course, grayish and fluttering in strips in the sneaking chilly wind there was up there. I could see a lot of his skin. It was white, corpse white, and it shone out against the rock and the fog almost as if it were luminous.

The chains he was locked up in—they *were* luminous. They were really queer. They shone. They were almost transparent, like glass, but whiter and stonier-seeming. A big link of the chain between his right arm and leg was lying on the rock just in front of me. I could see the grains of rock magnified through it, pink and black and gray and white, bigger through the middle of the link than at the edges, and with a milky look. It was like looking through a teardrop.

He didn't move. My strength came back a little, and I couldn't see him harming me in that state, so I got up and started to edge my way along the ledge in front of him to get at the water. When I was standing up, I was surprised to find how big he was. He was about half as big again as an ordinary man. And he wasn't quite dead. The white skin was up in goose-pimples all over him, with little shivers chasing across it. That was why I said what I did about Art, earlier on. He must have been frozen. But I could tell he was pretty far gone. He had a serious wound round on his left side, a bit below his heart. I hadn't seen it till then, and I didn't want to look at it when I did see it. It was a real mess, gaping and bleeding, with bits of his torn shirt fluttering across it and getting mixed up in it. No wonder he seemed to be dying.

I was almost right in front of him, trying not to look, when he moved his head and looked at me. "Be careful not to touch the chains," he said.

I jumped, and stared up at him. He didn't speak at all like someone who was dying. There was a bit of a shiver caught at him as he said it, but that was not surprising, considering how cold he must have been. But his voice was quite strong and he was looking at me like someone with sense. "Why mustn't I touch them?" I said.

"Because they're made to act like the Bounds," he said. "You won't get your drink if you do touch them."

I shuffled backwards an inch or so. I didn't dare go further, for fear of falling off the ledge. "What are they made of?" I said. "I've never seen anything like them before."

"Adamant," he said.

That is a sort of diamond—adamant—the

hardest thing there is. Granite must be almost the next hardest. I could see the big transparent staples driven into the granite on either side of him, holding him spread out. "You must be awfully strong, if it takes that to hold you," I said.

He sort of smiled. "Yes. But there was meant to be no mistake."

It looked that way to me too. I couldn't think why he was so much alive. "You're not a Homeward Bounder, are you?" I asked doubtfully.

"No," he said.

I went on staring at him, trying to keep from looking at that wound of his, and watching him shiver. I was cold myself, but then I could move about to keep warm. He was chained so that he could hardly move a foot in any direction. And all the while I stared, that water ran and poured, away to one side, with a long hollow poppling which had me licking my lips. And he was chained so he could hear it and not get to it.

"Are you thirsty?" I said. "Like me to get you a drink?"

"Yes," he said. "I'd welcome a drink."

"I'll have to get it in my hands," I said. "I wish I'd got something to hold it in."

I went edging and shuffling round him, keeping well away from the chains. I could see the stream by then, pouring down a groove in the rock, just beyond the reddish spiked thing that all the chains were hooked into. The ledge got narrower there. I was thinking that it was going to be difficult to climb over that spike on the slippery rock without touching a chain, when I realized what the spike was. I went close and leaned over it to make sure. Yes it was. An anchor. One spike was buried deep in the granite and all of it was orange wet rust, but there was no mistaking it. And all the chains led through the ring on the end of the shank.

I spun round so fast then that I never knew how I missed the chains. "*They* did this to you!" I said to him. "How did *They* do it? Why?"

He was turned to look at me. I could see he was thinking about water more than anything. I went climbing over the anchor to show him I hadn't forgotten. "Yes, it was *They*," he said.

I put my hands under the little pouring waterfall and filled them as full as I could with water. But I was so furious for him that my hands shook, and most of the water had trickled away by the time I'd climbed back over the anchor. Even more had gone by the time I managed to stretch my hands up to him among the chains, without touching one. He was so tall and chained so close that it was quite a struggle for him to get his mouth down. I don't think he got more than a taste the first time. But I went back and forwards, back and forwards, to the stream. I got quite nimble after a while. I even took a drink myself, after his sixth handful. He was so thirsty it was awful, and I kept thinking how he would feel if I happened to touch a chain and got twitched away just as he'd got his mouth down to the water.

"You should have asked me straight off," I said. "Why didn't you? Have *They* forbidden you to, or something?"

"No," he said. "*They* don't have that kind of power over me. But I could see how thirsty you were, and I'm more used to it than you."

"How long have you been here like this?" I said. We were talking this way as I went to and fro. "As long as the Flying Dutchman? Do you know him?"

He smiled. He was getting more cheerful as he drank, in spite of his situation. I just wished I'd had some food I could have given him too. "From long before the Dutchman," he said. "Long before Ahasuerus too. Almost from the beginning of the worlds."

I nearly said "I don't know how you stand it!" but there was no point in saying that. He had to. "How did *They* get you?" I said. "Why?"

"It was my own fault," he said. "In a way. I thought *They* were friends of mine. I discovered about the Bounds, and all the ways of the worlds, and I made the bad mistake of telling *Them*. I'd no idea what use *They* would make of the discovery. When it was too late, I saw the only safeguard was to tell mankind too, but *They* caught up with me before I'd gone very far."

"Isn't that just like *Them*!" I said. "Why aren't you hating *Them*? I do."

He even laughed then. "Oh I did," he said. "I

hated *Them* for aeons, make no mistake. But it wore out. You'll find that. Things wear out, specially feelings." He didn't seem sad about it at all. He acted as if it was a relief, not hating *Them* any more.

Somehow that made me hate *Them* all the worse. "See here," I said, reaching up with the tenth handful or so of water, "isn't there any way I can get you out of this? Can't I find an adamant saw somewhere? Or do the chains unlock anywhere?"

He stopped before he drank and looked at me, really laughing, but trying not to, to spare my feelings. "You're very generous," he said. "But *They* don't do things like that. If there's any key at all to these chains, it's over there." And he nodded over at the anchor before he bent to drink.

"That anchor?" I said. "When it's rusted away, you mean?"

"That will be at the ends of the worlds," he said.

I saw he was trying to tell me kindly not to be a fool. I felt very dejected as I shuffled off for the next handful of water. What could I *do*? I wanted to do something, on my own account as well as his. I wanted to break up his chains and tear the worlds apart. Then I wanted to get my hands on a few of *Their* throats. But I was simply a helpless discard, and only a boy at that.

"One thing I can do," I said when I came climbing back, "is to stay and keep you company and bring you water and things."

"I don't advise that," he said. "*They* can control

you still, to some extent, and there's nothing I can do to help you."

He had had enough to drink by then. He said I should go. But I sat down defiantly on the wet rock, shivering. Both of us shivered. The fog was blowing round us like the cold breath of giants. I looked up at him. He had his head leaned back again and that look on his face that was like peace but nearer death.

"Tell me the rules," I said. "You must know every rule there is, if you found out about them."

At that, his head came up and he looked almost angry. "There are no rules," he said. "Only principles and natural laws. The rules were made by *Them. They* are caught inside *Their* own rules now, but there's no need for you to be caught too. Stay outside. If you're lucky, you might catch *Them* up in *Their* own rules."

"But there is that rule that nobody can interfere with a Homeward Bounder," I said. I was thinking about the boy and the wagon. It still made me feel bad.

"Yes," he said. "There is, isn't there?"

Then neither of us said anything much for quite a long while. That's the trouble with misery, or cold. It absorbs you. I still wonder how he could manage to be so human under it. Except, I think, he wasn't human. Eventually, I put my shivering face up and asked if he'd like another drink.

He was looking off into the fog, rather intently, and shook his head slightly. "Not now, thank you. I think it's time for the vulture to come."

I don't know why, but I got the point at once. I suppose I had been wondering, deep down, what made that new-looking wound of his. I found I was standing up, looking from the wound to his face and feeling ill. "Can't I beat it off for you?"

"No," he said, quite severely. "You can't do things like that against *Them*, and you mustn't try. Why don't you go?"

I wanted to say that I'd stay—stay and hold his hand as it were—but I felt weak with horror. I couldn't say a thing.

"It's all right," he said. "It has nothing to do with you. But do go. It's nearly here."

I looked up where he was looking. And sure enough, moving among the moving mist, were the shadowy wings of a huge bird. It was quite near, flapping overhead, and I could see its beak and its naked pink head. I still meant to stay. I *know* I did. But I was so horrified to see the bird so near that I went crouching away sideways with one hand over my head, and fell over the anchor, with the other hand on the chains.

It was nothing like the twitch that takes you through a Boundary in the normal way. It was ten times more violent. Those chains were so cold they burned. But instead of sticking to me, the way freezing things usually seem to do, these flung me off themselves. I felt a sort of sizzling. Then I was crashing away backwards and finishing the fall I'd started, only much harder, onto a hard floor strewn with dead grass.

I lay there, winded, for a bit. I may have cried, I felt so sad. I could see I was in a big barn, a nice warm place smelling comfortably of hay. There was a great gray pile of hay to one side of me, almost up to the wooden rafters. I was a bit annoyed that I'd missed it and landed on the floor. I went on lying there, staring up at the sun flooding in through chinks in the roof and listening to mice or rats scuttling, but I was beginning to feel uneasy. Something was wrong. I knew it was. This barn ought to have been a peaceful place, but somehow it wasn't.

I got to my knees and turned to the door. And stuck there. The door was a big square of sunlight. Outlined in it, but standing in the shadows, much nearer to me than was pleasant, was someone in a long gray cloak. This one had the hood up, but it made no difference. I knew one of *Them* when I saw *Them*. My heart knocked.

"Get up," said the outline. "Come here."

Now, this was a funny thing—I needn't have done what he said. I knew I needn't. But I was too scared not to. I got up and went over. At first the cloaked outline seemed to shimmer against the sun, but, as I got closer, it was more wavery still, as if I'd had my knuckles pressed to my eyes before I looked at it.

"You have been to a forbidden place," said the wavery shape.

"So what?" I said. "I'm a free agent. I was told that rule."

"You will not go there again," was the answer, "unless you want to share the same fate."

"I don't have to do what you say," I remember starting to say—and then it all goes vague. I really do not remember the next minute at all. I know my mind was nearly a complete blank in the first part I do remember. I had forgotten who I was, why I was there and—the thing *They* wanted—where I'd just been. By that time, I had wandered in a dazed way out into the farmyard. The moment I remember is the moment the farmer came out of his cowshed and saw me.

"What do you think you're up to in there?" he roared at me. He was huge. He picked up a thick stick as huge as himself and came after me with it.

I ran. I was not too dazed for that. I ran, with my mind as numb as a foot that's gone to sleep, wondering what was happening and why. I swear I hadn't a thought or a memory in my head beyond that. Around me, chickens flapped and squawked and ran. Behind me, the farmer roared. And, beside me, just as I got to the farm gate, a huge dog plunged out of a kennel to the end of its rattling chain and almost got me.

That rattling chain. Even *They* don't think of everything. If *They* had thought to change it to a rope, I wouldn't be telling this tale now. I'd have forgotten. I could never hear a chain rattle after that without thinking of him, chained to his rock.

I cannoned into the gatepost and the dog just missed me. I made off down a muddy lane, remembering him on his rock at least. I thought, as I floundered along, that it had probably been a vision. Everything else in my head was vague, though it was coming back to me, in prickles, like your foot does when it stops being asleep. As I said, there are still times when I think he was a vision, but I try not to believe that, because I know *They* wanted me to. He was real. For that time, he was the only real thing I knew. It took days for the rest of my mind to come back. I had a terrible time too, because I had to start almost from scratch, as if I'd never been a Homeward Bounder before. And that was not an easy world to be a beginner in—believe you me! Thanks to *Them*, I never got to see the sign on the Boundary barn, but it didn't matter. I knew what it was. It was UNFRIENDLY.

After that, I traveled on. I was on near on a hundred worlds, wandering on and on. You wouldn't believe how tired you get. You just get settled, and get to know some of the people and some of their ways, and you find a job you can do, or a school that will have you—if it's that kind of strict world—and you're just getting used to it, when *bang*! up starts the dragging and the yearning, and you're on your way again. In the end, you never do get settled, because it's always at the back of your mind that you're going to move on.

I got to be past master at making my way in a world. I took pride in it. The knack is not to care too much. Treat it as a joke. I got so that I didn't care what I said, or how much I stole, or what dirty work I did. I found out that if people upped and blamed me, I could get out of trouble best by making them laugh. The only time this didn't work was when a solemn old priest tried to adopt me. Nothing would make him laugh. Nothing would make him believe I wasn't going to grow up into a priest too. He said he was going to save my soul. I only managed to get out of that when the Bounds were calling so strongly that I was near screaming.

Of course, the best way to get on in a new world would be to tell them you're a Homeward Bounder and why. But you find you can't do that. They don't believe you. Most of the time they think you're mad. Or they may believe that you're condemned to wander forever, but they never believe that you have to do it on more than their own world. And nothing will make anyone believe in *Them*. *They* make sure of that. If you start talking of *Them*, people cut you short and ask you what sin you were condemned for. They're always sure you've sinned if you talk about *Them*. And you find yourself inventing a suitable sin to satisfy them. On the few occasions I talked about it, my story was that I had spied on forbidden sacred mysteries. True enough, in a way.

I didn't talk about it much. I really didn't dare. After the way the Flying Dutchman had carried on about things not being permitted, and *Them* doing that to my mind straight after it, I was scared to say much even to other Homeward Bounders.

I met quite a lot of Homeward Bounders as time went on. You find the Bounds are quite crowded if you walk them long enough. Homeward Bounders always help one another. It stands to reason. We're usually very friendly to one another in a quick, jolly, shallow sort of way. We tell one another the jokes from our latest world, and help one another get set up in a new world if we happen to meet coming through a Boundary. But I never saw much point in confiding in any of them. You never meet the same one more than once. And, though they were all sorts and conditions of people—I've met kings and queens, crooks and artists, several actors and a six-foot lady who wrote sermons—they were one and all grown-up, and they all rather looked down on me for being only a boy.

It didn't matter. As soon as the Bounds called and I got to the Boundary with whomever it was, that was the end of the acquaintance. We both got twitched to different worlds. That seemed to be another rule. I hadn't known at first that a Boundary could send people to more than one place, but they can. And they always do. *They* can't have Homeward Bounders getting together. Oh no. That wouldn't do at all.

You wouldn't believe how lonely you get. I got so bad sometimes that I couldn't think of anything but Home. I remembered it over and over, those ordinary twelve years, until I felt it was plainer to me than when I lived there. I even used to dwell on the rows I had with Rob, and the way Rob and I used to tease Elsie. Elsie was good to tease, having ginger hair and a hot temper. I remembered her stamping and yelling, "I'm better at football than you! So!" Maybe she was better. She never kicked the ball into people's washing, the way I did. It would give me that cold foot ache inside, wanting to go back and play football in the alley again. I knew it was all there, just the same as I remembered, waiting for me to come back. I knew it must be. Otherwise I wouldn't still be a boy.

When I got really miserable, I found I couldn't help remembering him on his rock too. That always made me worse. He was still there too. I think I never hated *Them* as much on my own account as I did on his.

Anyway, that's enough of that. All I really meant to say was that I had been on a good hundred worlds before the next important thing happened. I had gone in a great slow circle, starting from the place where I nearly drowned, out and some way back again. If you walk the Bounds long enough, you get the feeling of where you've been, and I know that's what I'd done. I'd seen more kinds of worlds than you'd believe possible, more peculiar differences, and more samenesses than I like to think. I was a thoroughly hardened Homeward Bounder. There seemed nothing I didn't know.

Then I ran into Helen. My friendly neighborhood enemy. There really was nothing like Helen on any world I'd ever been to. I sometimes didn't think she was human at all.

V

It happened in a casual sort of way. I'd been landed on this real swine of a world. It really was the worst I'd ever been on. Everything about it was awful: the weather, the food, the local animals, and as for the people, they were not only brutes, but their habits were worse than that. It will show you when I say that no one lived in a house: they all lived in fortresses, half underground. Anyone outside a fortress was fair game. The *Them* playing it must have been right swine.

I was only on it a week. I've never been so glad when the Bounds called. I made haste through the pouring rain and sleet to get to the Boundary as fast as I could.

I'd still got half a mile to go—I could see something ahead through the lashing rain that had to be the Boundary—when the rain stopped. The sun came out for the first time since I'd been there. And it was typical of that beastly world that it got hotter than an oven in seconds. Instead of rain, the air was full of steam. It was like a hot fog. Worse than that, the mud I'd been wading through all that time dried out like ink on blotting paper. The water just sank away out of it and left me toiling through deep sand. I could hardly walk. I said some more of the bad words I'd been saying all that week. The Bounds were calling hard, and the slower you go the worse they get.

Then the steam cleared away like the mud had done. I was left floundering through a blazing white desert. It was so bright that I screwed my eyes almost shut and hunched in a heap. My bad words died away in a sort of moan. It was so hot and bright that it hurt.

Then I heard someone coming crunching quickly up behind me. In that world, you didn't let people come up behind you. I turned round, even though I was fairly sure this person must be another Homeward Bounder, and tried to open my eyes. Everything was blue-bright. I could only see the person as a black shape. The shape was about the same size that I was and seemed to have its back to me. I was so sure that this person was facing the other way that it gave me a real shock when the person said, "What are you waiting for? It's got to the hurry-hurry part," and went marching past me.

I turned round as the person went past, and there wasn't a face on the back of their head either. It seemed to be black hair all round. And whoever-it-was was marching so fast through the sand that I was quite ashamed. After all, the person was no bigger than I was.

I went hastening and ploughing after. It was really heavy going. "You don't have to hurry when it says so," I panted.

"I know I don't," snapped the person, marching swifter than ever.

"Then why—how do you manage to walk so fast in this sand anyway?" I gasped. Both my shoes were full of sand by then.

"Because I'm used to it," snapped the person. "I live here." And stopped and waited for me. I crunched and waded up very cautiously, thinking that this couldn't be a Homeward Bounder after all—in which case, on that world, watch out! And yet—and yet—Well, all I can say is that you get to know the look of a Homeward Bounder, and I still thought this was. "I am Haras-uquara," she said haughtily, when I got there. "My name is Helen in the language of the wider times."

"Mine's Jamie," I said, trying to look at her in the fierce sun. She must have a face, I decided, on the front of her head, in the usual way. I could just see the pointed brown tip of a nose poking out among the black hair there. But her hair really did seem to hang down the same way all round her head. She was dressed in black trousers and a black sweater and had black shoes with thick bouncy soles on her feet. Now the people in this world were a peculiar lot, but they always wore armor, and had their hair scraped back inside a helmet with a mirror-attachment so that they could see what was coming to attack from behind. And they spoke a croaking, gabbling language. She had spoken to me in English. "You can't come from here," I said. "You're speaking English."

"Of course," she said. "I saw you were a stranger and I spoke to you in the language of the wider times."

We began to shuffle towards the Boundary as she said this. You find you really have to go when they call.

"And you're a Homeward Bounder too?" I said, shuffling.

The tip of her nose stuck up disgustedly. "Is that what you call yourself? I'm an exile, condemned by the mouth of Uquar. They turned me out of the House of Uquar, and of course I got stoned. I'm angry."

She was lucky only to have been stoned, I thought. My eyes were watering in the sun, but I could see that her black clothes were splashed with sandy white mud all over. In some places there were holes, and she was bleeding a bit where the holes came. It looked as if she was telling the truth. "Why were you turned out?" I said.

"Because of *Them*," she said, with immense hatred.

I knew she was telling the truth. Only somebody new to the Bounds would talk about *Them* like that.

"*They* don't like you to talk about *Them*," I said.

"It's what I like, not what *They* like that matters," she said. "I'm not *Their* slave! I'm going freely into honorable exile. So there!"

"Why?" I said.

"Because of my gift," she said, and went stalking up the hill to the Boundary.

I suppose I should have let her go. She wasn't exactly friendly. But it narked me to see her going so fast while I floundered, and I knew that as soon as we got to the Boundary, we'd both be twitched off different ways and I'd never see her again. So I floundered hard and got to the top of the hill at the same time as she did. It was only a small Boundary. And it was typical of Helen's beastly world that it was marked out with bones.

They were great big bones, rib-bones like the skeletons of ships and leg-bones as high as lamp posts. I'd met one of the animals they came from three days before. I wasn't sure if it was a dragon or not, but it looked like one and it clearly thought I was good to eat. I only got away by hiding down the chimney of one of the fortresses. I don't think the dragon breathed fire, but it sniffed at the chimney for a good hour, until I was almost roasted from the fire down below.

"On holy days we bring a bone and plant it here," Helen explained.

I made a grunt and pushed past her to go inside the ring of bones. The white sand inside was criss-crossed with the black shadows of the bones. It took me an instant to see that the sand among the shadows was squiggling. I stopped at once and pretended to be getting the sand out of my shoes. It was not imagination, or the heat. The place was alive with snakes.

Helen came up beside me. I could feel she was disgusted at my cowardice. She clapped her hands, briskly and loudly. "Go away!" she said.

The sand among the shadows sort of seethed, and the snakes went. I could see them pouring out between the bones on the other side of the circle. "Thanks," I said. "Is that your gift?"

"Great Uquar, no!" she said. "Those were only snakes."

"I know," I said. "I didn't care to be stung."

"They don't sting. They bite," she said. "Shall I show you my gift?"

"If you want," I said, and I stepped into the circle of bones, meaning to be off elsewhere next second.

"As a great favor," she said. "Look."

When someone says "Look," you do. I looked in spite of the Bounds calling away. My eyes were getting used to the glare by then. Helen was rolling up the right sleeve of her black sweater. Her skin was a lot browner than mine, but her arm was an ordinary arm, bruised in one place and scratched in another.

"Snap!" I said. "Only mine's pinker."

A laugh came from behind Helen's sheet of black hair. The arm went gray. It started at Helen's fingers and grew gray the whole way up, and with every inch or so of grayness it grew a deep wrinkle, until it was gray and wrinkled right up to her shoulder. The skin of it seemed to get thick and dry, with just a few long black hairs growing on it. Where Helen's hand had been were a couple of fleshy points, with two pinker holes deep inside. This gray arm swung and curled up. I could see it hadn't any bone in it any longer.

I said, *"Eeeurgh!"* and backed away. As I did, the gray arm shot out suddenly to twice its length, almost straightening out all its wrinkles, and wrapped itself round my neck. It felt warm and leathery. *"Stop that!"* I said. I backed away and tried to untwist the warm gray snake from my neck, but it was unbelievably strong. It clung and clung. Helen thought it was ever so funny. She threw back her head, so that I almost saw face behind the hair, and laughed and laughed at me, and went on hanging on. I went on going backwards, pulling at the gray arm and shouting at her to stop it, and pulling Helen along with me because she wouldn't let go.

Then we got to the place where the twitch came. And we both went together. I was so surprised that I stopped shouting. There we were, both of us, in much mistier sunlight, which made me feel almost blind for a moment. Helen had difficulty seeing too. She had one hand up, parting her front hair a bit, and there was a bright black eye showing. She was watching her gray arm turn brown and smooth again, from the shoulder downwards. I recognized it as it began to vanish.

"That's an elephant's trunk!" I said. "How did you do that?"

"That's my gift," she said. "I can just do it. Where are we?"

"In another world," I said. I looked round while I was tipping the sand out of my shoes and began to feel regretful. We were not going to be here long, and it looked really inviting. We were in an open space in a tropical sort of forest. Everything was unbelievably bright and fruitful. The green, green trees were hung with bunches of fruit and draped with creepers growing blue and white flowers as big as plates. The only reason I didn't find this hot sun dazzling was because I'd just been in the desert in Helen's world. It was the kind of sun that brings scents and colors out. The place smelled wonderful. It was quiet, except for one or two peaceful rustlings. I took that to be squirrels or monkeys. There weren't any birds singing, but that is not the kind of thing you notice after Helen's world. "This is a jungle," I said to Helen.

"I can see that," she said. "What do we do? Can we eat any of that fruit?"

"It's better not to try," I said.

The tip of the nose came out of the black hair and pointed haughtily at me. "We can't die. I was told that."

"Then you were lucky. You were told more than I was," I said. "But I've eaten things that made me sorry I *couldn't* die, before I learned to be careful."

"Then say what we *do*," said the haughty tip of nose.

I was quite annoyed by then. She was so superior. Who was she, just new to the Bounds, to behave this way *and* play a silly trick on me? I had ten times her experience. I set out to show her. "The best thing," I said patronizingly, "is not to eat until you see what the natives are eating. We're not going to be here long—"

"I can tell that," she snapped.

"—So we needn't eat at all," I said. I was mad. "Yes, you'll find you get a feeling about how long you're going to be in a place. You're coming on very nicely. The next thing to do is to go and look for any marks that other Homeward Bounders have left. There's a sort of path over there. The signs should be in a tree near it."

I led the way loftily over to a bushy sort of opening at the edge of the clearing. I looked knowingly up and around. There was a sign. It was slashed into the trunk of a tree that looked like a huge fern. And—this would have to happen!—it was one I didn't know.

"There it is," I said, pointing to it, trying to think what I should say next. "It's a very rare sign, that is."

Helen's nose pointed up to it. "You don't know what it means."

"Yes, I do," I said. "It means VERY PLEAS-ANT WORLD. Those are very rare."

"Yes," she said. "Then what?"

"We go and look for some natives," I said, "but carefully, not to alarm them. I should think they'd be rather primitive in a place like this."

We set off down the path. It was like a green tunnel, with fruit and huge flowers hanging down and brushing our heads.

"Suppose these natives of yours speak a different language," Helen said. "What do we do?"

"Learn it," I said gloomily. "But don't worry. I know hundreds of languages by now. An awful lot of them are quite alike. You let me do the talking and we'll be all right."

We went on a while, and then Helen seemed to decide to pick my brains. She said, "These signs you people with the stupid name have for one another—what are the commonest?"

"Warnings mostly," I said. "Things like SLAVERS OPERATE HERE or POLICE TAKE BRIBES or DON'T OFFEND THE PRIESTS or UN-FRIENDLY. Yours had OUCH! which just about sums it up, to my mind."

"There's no need to be rude," she said. "It's my Home. I shall go back there before long, you'll see." That made me smile. It was just what I'd thought. "What's the most uncommon sign?" she said. "That one back there?"

I thought it must be, since I had never seen it

before. "Not quite," I said, so as to seem to know best. "The one I was told was most uncommon is YOU CAN TELL THEM YOU'RE A HOME-WARD BOUNDER."

"Why?" she said.

"Because you can't," I said. "*They* make sure people don't believe you."

"So then the sign never happens!" she said scornfully.

"Yes it does," I said. "It was in the list I was given. It must happen somewhere."

"Of course it must," Helen said pityingly. She was like that. She'd say first one thing, and then contradict it with the opposite, and make it seem that it was you who were wrong. "The wider times have every possibility in them, so there must be a traverse where you can admit to your exile. That is the logic of Uquar—"

"What kind of talk is that?" I said.

She wasn't listening. "Uquar," she said furiously, "is an utter cheat! I don't think he exists!"

"Who is he anyway?" I was saying, when we came to the bushy edge of the jungle. There was a man standing in a bush at the side of the path, bowing and smiling at us. He didn't look uncivilized. He was clean-shaven and wearing a neat whitish shirt and trousers, and the smile on his face was a polite, social sort of smile. He looked so harmless that I turned to Helen and said loftily, "Let me handle this." I bowed to the man. "Good afternoon, my friend."

He answered in a language I had never heard before. "Oomera-woomera-woomera," he went.

I think my face looked pretty funny. Snorting noises came from behind Helen's hair. "It doesn't matter," I told her. "We make signs."

The man made the signs. He bowed and stretched out one hand. He was saying, "Will you come this way, sir?" like the waiters in a restaurant where I once worked. So I nodded and Helen jerked her head. She always nodded in a sideways jerk that looked as if it meant No. It took some getting used to. But the man seemed to understand. He was very pleased. He ushered us politely along a road, between fields. There were more neatly clothed men and some boys working in the fields with long hoes, but they downed tools when they saw us and came hurrying along with us, beaming and going "Oomera-woomera-woomera" too. It was like being royalty, except that it was friendlier. I happened to look round, and there were more neat men hopping out of the jungle and rushing after us with glad "oomera-woomeras."

Beyond the fields, we came to the village. That was neat and civilized too. All the houses were square and painted white, with pretty, decorated trellises up the fronts, and shiny brass pots standing by their neatly painted front doors. They were built round three sides of a square, and at the back of the square was a bigger white building with bigger trellises, which seemed to be the village hall. They led us to this hall across the square, through the friendliest welcome I've ever had in my life. The girls and women joined in here, beaming and smiling and clattering the rows and rows of turquoise beads they wore over their long whitish dresses. They were all rather gushing types, these women. One came up to Helen, with her arms stretched out, cooing "oomera-woomera," and put her hands out to part the hair in front of Helen's face.

The piece of Helen's face I saw looked as if it were going to bite. She jumped back and shouted, *"Don't do that!"*

I've been on numbers of worlds where people keep their faces hidden. I wasn't sure why Helen did, unless it was this Haras-uquara thing she was, and I'd never seen anyone use quite Helen's method before, but I always think you should respect customs. "Oomera-woomera," I said to the surprised woman. "You mustn't do that. Her face is sacred." The woman nodded and backed away, making *so-sorry* signs.

I thought Helen should have been grateful, but she said, "There's no need for you to be rude too!"

She was in a very bad temper after that—if you can put it that way, when she hadn't been in a good one yet. We were taken to seats on piles of cushions at one end of the hall and we were given a feast. We were guests of honor with a vengeance. I only had to look at any of the food they brought for it to be heaped into the brass pot they gave me as a plate.

Everyone smiled and cheered and oomera'd and nodded, and more and more food came in: smoking brass buckets of bean hash, piles of rice, bits of stuff wrapped in leaves with hot sauce poured on top, pancakes and bread-cakes and fruity savory pies. And twenty kinds of salad. And piles of every kind of fruit I'd seen in the jungle. It was all delicious. The only drawback was that it was all vegetarian stuff. I do like a bit of meat myself.

Helen hardly touched it. She sat with her head hanging so that even the tip of her nose was invisible and behaved as if her face was too sacred to put food in. I think what had happened was that it had hit her for the first time what being a Homeward Bounder meant, but I don't know. I never knew what Helen was thinking.

"Do eat," I said. "You'll offend them. You're guest of honor."

"You eat for me," she said. "You stuff. I don't want any. I don't like this place. I wish I could go Home."

So I ate away, trying to make up for Helen. After a bit, they cleared all the food away and brought hot drinks. I was glad. I was too full to be happy by then.

You can imagine my dismay when, after the drinks, out came the brass pots again, and in came a whole lot more food. This course was a mass of things on sticks—all vegetables—and corn on the cob and suchlike. Stacks of it. And I had to have something of each. They insisted on it. That's the worst of not knowing the customs. You don't know how to pace yourself. I'd already eaten too much anyway.

"I remember my mother going on about eating for two," I said to Helen, "before my sister Elsie was born. I'd no idea it was such hard work!"

"You're eating like a pig for the slaughter!" said the voice under the hair.

"I am not! I'm being polite," I said.

Then they took the things on sticks away and brought in puddings. Piles of puddings. I was nearly bursting by then. But I went on doggedly. You have to respect customs. There was no pleasure in it. I was afraid I was going to be sick. I had to refuse two of the rice puddings. I've never been so glad to see a meal over as I was when that one was finished. Everyone got up at last. I got up too, feeling like a vast, fat cushion with little tiny arms and legs at the corners. I could hardly walk to the place where we were to sleep. It was a small square room at the back of the hall, filled with cushions almost as stuffed as I was. They shut the door and went away and I stood there. I couldn't sit down or even move, I was so full.

It was almost dark in there. The only light was a little blue lamp in the ceiling. Helen was stumbling about behind me, but I couldn't see what she was doing, because I daren't turn round even. Finally, she came and sat with a flounce on the cushions where I could see her.

"Well!" she said. "Well!" She put her hands up,

parted the hair where her nose came through, and hooked each side behind her ears. I supposed she could do that because it was so dark, but I didn't really care. My mind was all on my overcrowded stomach. The sacred face was a fierce pointed brown face with round shiny black eyes, like observant buttons. "You've got us into a nice mess!" she said. "The door's locked. What did you say that sign on the tree meant, again?"

I couldn't speak. Things were surging inside.

"I'll tell you," Helen said. "It came to me when I said you were stuffing like a pig for the slaughter. And I knew. That sign means CANNIBALS. Haven't you noticed that there aren't any animals here, not even hens?"

The surging turned out to be a huge gurk. I gave it. It was double-barreled. Relief! I could speak. "They're vegetarians," I said.

"When they can't get meat," said Helen. "When there are no stray travelers. We're the meat. There'll be an even bigger feast tomorrow, I'll bet you. Meat patties, meat balls, steak, mince and stew."

"Oh shut up!" I said. Things were still critical inside. "Homeward Bounders can't die. You know that."

"In that case," said Helen, "how will it feel to go on living inside a whole village?"

"Shut *up*!" I said. "I don't think they could. There's this rule that something awful happens to people who harm Homeward Bounders. Rule Two."

"Will that help us," Helen said musingly, "if they decide to eat us a leg or an arm at a time?"

"Will you be quiet!" I said. "You are making me sick, and I don't need your help for that at the moment! It's not true. You're guessing."

"Then why are you so cross?" she said.

She had me there. I had to admit it. I thought she was right. It was creepy how glad they were to see us. And now the door was locked. "All right," I said. "I'm sorry. I didn't know what that sign meant. I'd never seen it before."

"That's what annoys me," she said. "I was afraid you were a fool and now I know you are. I wouldn't have bothered to bring you with me if I'd known. I'd be better off on my own."

That took my breath away. The cheek! The cool cheek! "So you were just making use of me!" I snarled. "You and your elephant's trunk!"

"Well, yes," she said, as cool as a cucumber. "I was trying it out. I knew that a traverse casts in all directions, so that two or more people fly outwards from one another. Those were the words they taught it to me in, but it doesn't feel like flying, does it? More like a twitch. And I thought that if two people were holding on to one another, then it was *likely* they'd go together. So I decided to hang on to you as soon as I saw you. I could see you didn't belong in our world, so that meant you'd had some experience in exile. I thought you'd make a native guide for me. Instead, you get us both eaten. I wish I'd left you alone now."

"I swear to you," I said, "I've never been in a fix like this before. Ever. How do you come to know so much about the Bounds anyway?"

"From being brought up in the House of Uquar," said Helen. "Because of my gift. I told you. When I was old enough, my word was to have run throughout the world. Now I shall have to wait until I can get back. It's all *Their* fault! I shall find a way to make *Them* suffer for it too!"

"You really mustn't talk about *Them* like that," I said nervously. "I think *They* know."

"I'm sure *They* do," said Helen. "And *They're* welcome to listen if *They* wish. I intend to talk about *Them*. You can put your fingers in your ears if you're scared, but I'm going to tell you all the same."

And tell me she did. After the way she'd said it, I'd have died rather than put my fingers in my ears and, anyway, I was too interested. My stomach suddenly went thinner a little after that. I squatted opposite her on the cushions and we talked half the night.

VI

Helen had been born with her right arm just a withered stump. Her mother was very sad about it, because in that world you don't get far if you don't have two hands. From my experience there, I'd say that if you happened to have an extra pair on top of that, you'd still only just be holding your own. It's every man—or woman—for himself there. Life is a perpetual stalking ambush. You don't go out shopping, you go out robbing—and then get robbed yourself on your way home with the robberies. And on top of that there are the dragon-things, snakes, tigers and savage great birds to peck you to death.

So Helen's father was going to sling her out of their fort. A new baby wouldn't have lasted five minutes outside, but he said it was kindest. Helen's mother wept and cried and begged, and in the end she persuaded him to keep Helen for a six month's trial as it were. And when Helen was four months old—you know, the sort of time when babies start holding up their hands and staring at them and going *goo-ga* at their fingers—Helen began holding up her left hand, because that was the only one she'd got. And she looked at it very seriously. Then she looked very seriously and carefully at her mother's hands when her mother came to play *goo-ga* with her too. And the next time her mother came, Helen had a right arm, almost like an ordinary baby, except that, not having much to compare it with, she'd got the hand wrong. It was a left hand, with the thumb where the little finger should be. Her mother thought she was dreaming at first, and didn't say anything, because there were still two months to go. And by the time Helen was six months old, she'd put the hand right and had a perfect pair of arms like an ordinary baby.

Helen's father bore her a grudge for proving him wrong. People were like that in that world. In revenge, he sent off an armed messenger to the House of Uquar to ask if this was natural, or should he kill Helen out of hand, as it were?

The House of Uquar, as far as I could work out, was a sort of cross between a temple and a university and an army headquarters. It was the one place in the world nobody dared rob. And it was very much respected because—I think—Uquar was a sort of god. The people there got very excited and sent out an armored column to have a look at Helen. Helen said she remembered them, even though she was only a baby. She remembered the head Hand of Uquar poking at her right hand with a sort of stick, and poking again, until in the end she got angry and turned her arm into a stick too and poked back at him. And they were very impressed.

"He said it wasn't a deformity at all," Helen told me. "It was the manifestation of the Hand of Uquar at last. They'd been waiting centuries for it. They said that when I grew up I would hold sway over the whole world, and bring back the wider times, because that was the prophecy. I was to come and be brought up in the House of Uquar when I was five, and be called Haras-uquara."

Helen's father couldn't wait to get rid of her. He was very peeved to have to keep her for another four and a half years, and he kept telling her that her arm *was* a deformity, whatever the Hand of Uquar said. When the time came for her to go to the House of Uquar, he sent her off with hardly any guard at all.

"He was right of course," Helen said. "It *is* a deformity, even though I call it a gift. I don't remember the journey very well. I don't think much happened. And I arrived safe and sound at the House of Uquar."

There was a great deal of learning at the House of Uquar. From what Helen said, I got to suspect that Helen's world was not always the horrible place I found it. They had a whole lot of knowledge left over from what they called these "wider times" and they were quite sure the "wider times" were going to come again once Helen was grown up. In those times everything was much more peaceful, including the weather, and her people had found out all sorts of things in those days that most other worlds still don't know. They found out about the ways of the worlds and the Bounds. When things began to get worse and worse, they built the House of Uquar like a huge fort and kept the knowledge there. They believed that when the "wider times" came again, everybody would be able to walk the Bounds, not just Homeward Bounders. That was why Helen was brought up to speak the language I call English.

Maybe that was reasonable. It is a fact that a lot of people seem to speak it, on a lot of worlds. But they knew in the House of Uquar that it wasn't the only language. Helen was made to learn a lot of others. She spoke some to me. And most of them were languages I'd had to learn as I went. Did I feel a fool! By this time, I was wondering why she thought she needed me as a native guide at all.

"Of course I do," she said. "My knowledge is just theory. You've done it."

"Theory's not such a bad thing," I said. "I'd no idea two people could go to the same place through a Boundary. I thought it was a rule they couldn't."

Helen's hair had been sliding down over her face as she talked. She jerked her head up crossly as I said that, letting out her nose and her two button eyes. "There are no rules," she said. "Only principles and natural laws."

"Who said that to you?" I said, quick and sharp. It was just what he had said—him chained to his rock.

"They were always saying that to me in the House of Uquar," Helen said, and her hair fell down across her face like a couple of curtains across a window. "It's the underlying principle. It must be *Them* who pretend there are rules."

It was a miracle I didn't start to tell her about him on his rock. It really was the luckiest thing—though I didn't know it. My head was full of him because of what Helen had said, and the last sight of him I'd had, looking up at that great bird as if he was dreading it. And I remembered him saying that he'd set out to tell mankind about the ways of the worlds. I had a strong idea he must have made a start and told them in Helen's world, before *They* got at him and stopped him.

The reason I didn't ask Helen about it was her darned hair. It was really annoying me by this time. "Why do you keep putting your face inside your hair?" I said. "Is it because of being Haras-uquara?"

There was a nasty silence. Then Helen said, "None of your business. I like it this way." And that was all I could ever get out of her about her hair. I think it may have been the truth.

After that it took some time to get her friendly again. I had to work at it. There were still so many things I wanted to know. "Let's get back to natural laws and stuff," I said, after about half an hour of soothing. "I think I must have got the Boundaries a bit wrong." And I told her about the circle of worlds I'd first got stuck on. "I always seemed to get to the

same ones in the same order," I said. "And another
thing, each of these Boundaries seemed to have only
three Bounds. I came up to most of them three
different ways by the end."

"You must have been very unlucky," Helen said.
"Traverses—Boundaries—vary as much as worlds
do. You obviously got caught in a triple circuit.
That's the smallest kind there is. If there had been
four of you using the traverses, there would have
been only three ways for you all to go, and two of
you would have flown off the same way."

"I'd have had company then, at least," I said.
"Do you tell the size of a Boundary from the number
of Bounds, then?"

"No," she said. "Only triple ones. Or total
traverses. You can go anywhere from them, and the
lines lie to them from all directions."

"RANDOM, do you mean?" I said.

"I don't know," said Helen. "You seem to have
got different words foreverything."

"They're the ones all Homeward Bounders use,"
I said. "But I don't think any of us understand the
ways of the worlds."

"Let me tell it you the way I was taught," said
Helen. Her face came poking out of her hair again. I
took that for a good sign. Actually it wasn't, not
always. Sometimes she put her hair back in order to
go for you better. But this time it was friendly-meant.

"You have sat down in a place of glass," she said.
"Glass is all round you, and the place is dark. Now,

light a light inside your place of glass. All round you, at once, there are reflections, going back infinitely, until your glass place is multiplied many times over. That is like the worlds, in a way. Except that it is not, because now you have to imagine other people in the reflections of your glass place, and lights lit on the outside of your place of glass too, so that you can see these lights reflected, outside and inside also, over and over again, along with your own place. By now there are myriads, all shining and overlapping, and you do not know which is real. This is the way of the worlds. All are real, lights and reflections alike. We pass from one to another, like light."

Helen stopped and thought a bit. "Except," she said, "that no one these days can pass through the glass. I was given two explanations of that. One is that, in the midst of all the lights, you sit in your place of glass, and this you know to be real. So it is the Real Place. But the other explanation was that, in the midst of the multiplicity of worlds, there is a true Real Place, known to be real by Uquar. They told me Uquar lived in the Real Place."

She stopped again. She was suddenly furiously angry. "I don't believe in the Real Place! I don't believe in Uquar any more! Everyone talked about Uquar, but no one mentioned *Them*. I think *They* have been pretending to be Uquar all these years, and deceiving everybody! But I saw *Them*. I saw what *They* were doing. *They* can't deceive me anymore! *They* were half hidden by the reflections of the House of Uquar and other worlds, so that it was dim and whitish over *Them*, but I saw. And I knew. And I was very, very angry!"

She raved on for quite a bit. What had happened, I think, was that Helen had been sent for by one of her teachers in the House of Uquar, and the teacher was busy when Helen arrived. Helen was not one of those who likes to hang about waiting. She had wandered crossly off into a bit of the House of Uquar she had never seen before. It was a huge place, by her account. And she had come upon a part—a sacred part, I think—where the wall seemed to her like a big misty window. Behind the window, she had seen *Them* at work on *Their* machines. And, being Helen, she had gone and pressed her pointed nose to the window and pushed her hair aside to see. *They* had turned and looked at her, but Helen hadn't cared. She had gone on staring through the reflections until she was certain what *They* were doing.

"And I was angry," she said. "*They* had our whole world spread out, on a table, and were moving people about in it, playing a game with us! Seven or eight or more of *Them*, using us as counters!"

"Seven or eight?" I said. "Mine only had two."

"There are games you can play round a board," said Helen, "or with cards. Some as many as ten can play. *They* were playing that kind of game with us! And I was angry, because I knew *They* had brought the floods, and the deserts, and the dinosaurs upon us, and turned us into bandits for *Their* pleasure!"

When Helen's teacher had come to look for her, she had seemed to think Helen was pointing angrily at a bare wall. From what Helen said, it seemed quite certain that none of her teachers could see *Them*. They were all puzzled and worried.

Almost straight after that, Helen was hauled up in front of the main Hand of Uquar. He had said, "My dear, the time has come for the second part of your training. You must now go forth as an exile and traverse the worlds until you have learned enough to expiate your sin."

He looked miserable about it. Helen said, "Why? What sin?"

"You have blasphemed against Uquar," he said.

"Yes, I have," said she. "I don't think he exists."

"No, no," he said. "You have called the gift of your hand a deformity."

"Yes, I did," she said. "But that isn't why you're sending me, is it? When are *They* going to allow me to come back?"

"You will find yourself back Home," he said. "And that will be a sign that your sin is expiated." And he had told her what to expect at the Boundaries—traverses, as they called them. They knew a lot there.

"So then," Helen said, "I told him straight that I was glad to go. I'd rather be an exile than a piece in a game played by *Them*. But he didn't listen."

"People don't," I said. "My exile was quite

different. *They* did it *Themselves*, and *They* told me *They* were discarding me to the Bounds for being a random factor."

"That makes it sound much more like a game," Helen said. "But *They* won't find it's a game when I start on *Them*. I'm not having my world used this way!"

She was still raving about it when I went to sleep. Maybe she went to sleep in the end too. But both of us sprang awake early in the morning. The Bounds were calling. It was an awful feeling. We got up and flung ourselves at the door, but it was tight locked and hardly even rattled.

"What do we *do*?" Helen said. It was almost the closest to panic I ever saw her. "What happens if we don't get to the Boundary?"

"I don't know," I said. "I told you I've never been in a fix like this before!"

"And it's all your fault," she said, and she went away and sat down again.

There was nothing else to do, really, but I couldn't sit down. The call was too strong. I stood leaning against the door, feeling it drag at me, and— believe it or not—I was starving hungry too. The more you eat, the hungrier you seem to get the next morning. Between the Bounds and starvation, I was in an awful state.

It was a good two hours before they opened the door. The moment they did, I toppled out backwards. The people outside caught me and held me pretty tight, and others went in for Helen. But these stopped suddenly and backed away. I looked round to see why.

Helen was covered in spiders. She must have spent most of the night collecting them. She was kind of gray and crawly with long spidery legs and short spidery legs, and little round spider bodies of every color from pale gray to black. There were a couple of webs too, between the top of her head and her shoulders. She stood up, and all the women coming for her backed away. It was pretty uncanny. But Helen said, talking to the spiders, "You'd better go away now." And they did, just as the snakes did in the Boundary. They ran down her from all sides and scuttled across the floor in crowds. The women held their skirts close to their legs and squeaked a bit.

"Stupids," Helen said. "Spiders don't hurt." Then she let herself be taken away. There was not much else either of us could do. There was most of the village there. And Helen had been right. No one was nodding and smiling now. They were just businesslike.

I don't know what happened to Helen. My lot took me to a bathroom sort of place, where they made sure I was thoroughly washed. I suppose they liked their meat hygienic. Then they gave me one of their neat whitish suits. I didn't mind that. My old clothes had been pretty beaten up in Helen's world.

All the time, the Bounds called, harder every minute. The result was that I kept trying to get away.

I made pointless dash after pointless dash. I was so desperate that I didn't care if Rule Two got them for interfering with me. And they caught me each time, firm and businesslike, as if they were used to it. The final time they grabbed me, they led me out of the hall and through the square towards the jungle. I felt almost better. That was the way the Bounds were calling me. The only two things I had to worry about then were how to get something to eat, and how not to *be* something to eat. And what had happened to Helen, of course.

I needn't have worried about Helen. We came in a crowd along the jungle path to that very selfsame clearing where the Boundary was, and the women came along with us, bringing Helen. I never found out what had gone on, but I don't think they had managed to bathe Helen. They certainly hadn't managed to change her clothes. She was still in the same muddy black outfit. She still didn't look as if she had a face. And there was a huge snake wrapped round her shoulders, hissing and rearing at people. Everyone was keeping a rather respectful distance. I thought at first that the snake was another trick of hers with that arm. But it wasn't. It was a real snake.

The next bit was bad. They kept us surrounded, at the edge of the clearing, and we were both nearly frantic to get to the Boundary in the middle. But they wouldn't let us move from beside a post they had set up by the trees. That post was one of the nastiest things I have ever seen. The top of it was carved and painted into a cluster of cruel little faces. All the faces were eating one another. Painted blood ran down the faces and down the post. Underneath the post stood the polite, social man who had been standing in the bush to meet us the day before. He didn't look social at all. He looked pleased. He was stripped to the waist and, in his hand, he was hefting a nice sharp brass hatchet.

"It may be all right," I said to Helen, not really believing it. "Something bad's bound to happen to him if he goes for us with that chopper."

"Yes," she said. "But he'll have chopped us in two by then. Take hold of my hand and run when I tell you."

I wasn't too keen to get near that snake of Helen's, but I moved over and took hold of her left hand. The snake put its tongue out at me, but otherwise took no notice. Helen used her right hand to part her hair and took a long careful look up at that nasty post. Then she stretched her right arm into the air and made it turn into the same carving as the post. Only hers was alive.

Each of her fingers budded into a cruel little head, and each as it budded turned and bit the next one. The palm of her hand swelled into two more heads, and her wrist into three, all gnawing away with white fangs. Blood—it looked real blood—was running down her arm before it began to turn into a post, and it went on running as the cruel mouths chewed. Helen turned it this way and that. Everyone near backed away, appalled—and I didn't blame them. It made me forget I was hungry, that thing.

As soon as a space was cleared, the snake unwrapped itself from Helen and slid to the ground, which made everyone back away further. The only one who didn't was the man with the hatchet. He came for us.

"Run!" Helen shouted.

And we did run, like mad for the middle of the clearing, with Helen holding her horrible arm over her head and the man leaping behind, swinging his hatchet. What he thought when we vanished, I don't know. We were in the middle of a carnival the next second.

That's the trouble with Boundaries. You often don't have time to catch your breath. I was still thinking I was going to be chopped in two any second, when I was being whirled away in a dance by a big white rabbit with balloons bobbing over his head. Other strange figures were dancing and laughing all round me. I tried to keep my head and hang on to Helen in the crowd, but she was far more confused than I was, and she let go. It took me ages to shake off the rabbit. I thought I'd lost her. I went fighting my way through the laughing, dancing, dressed-up crowd in a panic. Carnival music was stomping and hooting in my ears, and people kept swinging me round to dance, or handing me pies and toffees and oranges, and it really was only by the merest luck I found her. She was sitting on the steps of the bandstand, shaking her right hand and wringing its fingers.

"I hope I don't have to do that again," she said to me, just as if I had been there all along. "That hurt."

"I bet it did," I said. "Thanks. Have a toffee."

"You may well thank me," Helen said, but she took the toffee. "If you get us into another mess like that, I shall go away and leave you in it. What do we do now?"

"Have fun," I said, "by the looks of it."

We did have fun in that world. We called it Creema di Leema when we talked about it afterwards, because of the drink that made everyone so happy there. It was like a sort of creamy orange juice. It never made you really drunk — just happy and bubbly. We drank it of course. Everyone did there, from babies. You couldn't *not* drink it. They forced it on you. I think the *Them* playing old Creema di Leema thought it would be funny to have everyone a little drunk all the time. Anyway, it was one of the best worlds I've ever been in — like a month-long party.

Being a bit tanked up all the time, I started being as rude to Helen as she was to me. It turned out to be the right way to treat her. We slanged one another all the time. I stopped being afraid of her — I admit I was, up to then: she was so weird. And it helped that, in Creema di Leema, she was always making mistakes. She wasn't quite so capable as she seemed, and she really didn't understand the serious way they took their jollity there. She had been brought up too solemn.

A lot of her mistakes had to do with this power she had over creepy-crawlies. She always said that wasn't a gift: she just loved critters. And she did love them. If I'd had a row with Helen and I ever wanted to soothe her down, the surest way to do it was to find a worm or an earwig or a rat and give it her. She would hook her hair behind her ears and bend over the thing, beaming. "Oh isn't it beautiful!" she would say.

"No it isn't," I would say. "I just gave it you to keep you happy."

The trouble is, on a world of drunks, you have to go carefully with the snakes and spiders—and with the elephant trunks, for that matter. Old people didn't find them funny. In old age, they had taken enough Creema di Leema on board to start seeing snakes where no snakes were. They didn't take kindly to real ones.

Helen and I got a job as the front and back halves of a pantomime horse. We did a turn nightly on the Esplanado di Populo while the acrobats changed costume. We never could keep in step with one another, but that was supposed to be funny. They could hear us counting, "One, two—one, two—*change* step—no the left foot, you fool!" and fell about laughing.

After a week we had earned enough money to

get Helen some clothes. We had to go from shop to shop for them, because almost no one on Creema di Leema wears black, and Helen insisted on it. But she got them in the end, by sheer persistence. After another week, I was able to change my cannibal clothes too—I hated them by then. Mine were a nice dark bright red all over. The shop people thought they were just as sober as Helen's.

Helen celebrated my new getup by acquiring a bright red and black slippery snake I didn't know about. She included it that night in her end of the horse—the back end. It made itself known to me by getting up the back of my red shirt. I came half out of the front of the horse, red in the face and swearing horribly. The audience shrieked with laughter, until I managed to shake the blessed snake out of my clothes and it went whizzing across the stage into the crowd. Then they just shrieked.

"It was *not* a snake!" Helen yelled at me. "It's a kind of lizard."

"I don't care! You're not to do that again!" I bawled. "Get back in your horse. *Left*, right—*left*, right."

But they booed us off the stage. We nearly lost our job over it.

Another of Helen's mistakes happened when I'd let her be the front end of the horse for a change. She said it wasn't fair, not being able to see. From the front of the horse you could see quite well, out through its mouth. Helen stood in the middle of the stage and stared at the audience.

"Keep your mind on your job!" I growled at her. You get hot and nasty all wrapped in horse and bent down with your arms wrapped round the person in front.

But Helen gave a squeal and ran for the edge of the stage. It took me by surprise. I sat down and brought Helen's half of the horse down on top of me. She kicked to get free but she couldn't. The audience loved it. I didn't.

"Let me get up!" Helen yelled. "That's my mother in the audience! I haven't seen her since I was five!"

She got up and rushed to the front of the stage. I was still sitting down, so I was dragged along behind her. "No it isn't!" I shouted as I slid along. "Stop it! Listen! It can't be your mother!"

Luckily, the audience thought it was the funniest thing they had seen when the horse broke in half and the head turned angrily round to face the rear end. "What do you mean?" snapped Helen. "It *is* my mother!"

"No it isn't. Shut up!" I whispered. "Your mother's in your world. She must be, because she can't walk the Bounds. This is someone your mother would have been if she'd been born here instead. She may even have a daughter like you here, but I hope not for her sake!"

"I don't believe you," said Helen.

"Think about it," I said. "You know the ways of

the worlds better than I do." I told her how I'd met the printer who was a hairy herdsman in the cattle world. "Anyway," I said, "you'll frighten the poor woman to death if you go rushing up to her as half a horse. Then the horse opens, and a thing like *you* pops out. She'd have a stroke. Now shut up. You'll get us booed again."

"All right," Helen said sulkily. "I believe you. But you're still wrong."

The front half of the horse turned and backed into the back half—pretty hard: Helen usually gave at least as good as she got—and the show went on. Helen was in her worst mood for days after that. Not that I blame her. It would upset me to meet my mother like that too. In fact, it made me think of my Home then, as hard as Helen was evidently thinking about hers. We could hardly be civil to one another for days.

But we were good friends enough when the Bounds called again for me to hang on to Helen as we went to the Boundary. I'd got so that I'd feel lost without someone to be rude to.

VII

It was about an hour before dark when we made our next move. We were both sorry to go. The Esplanada was just starting to liven up for the night. Crowds of happy people were drifting about, offering one another swigs of Creema di Leema, and the colored lights were coming on. They looked particularly good, because the sky was yellow, with white stars pricking in, and the rows of red and green and blue lights swung against the yellow. We had a last nip of Creema when the call came and drifted up the Esplanada. As I said, I kept tight hold of Helen's sleeve. We didn't know quite where the Boundary was here, and I was taking no chances.

"We shall be quite well off," Helen said. "I've got lots of money."

"Then give it away," I said. "People will just laugh at it in the next place. Nothing varies so much as money. About the only thing that seems valuable all over is gold."

We passed money out in handfuls to any children we came to. In exchange, we got two balloons each, one of those whistles that blows out a long paper tube with a pink feather on the end, and a bag of sherbert sweets. We hadn't meant to make an exchange. But Creema people are like that.

And we couldn't have collected a more unsuit-able set of objects. The twitch took us just opposite the bandstand and landed us in the middle of a war. We saw the same yellow sky, with the same pricking stars. The lights were gone of course, and it was open country, with bushes where there had been houses. As we arrived, there was a yammering over to the right and a row of angry red twinkles. Little things went whining *phwee* overhead.

"Get down!" I said, and pulled Helen and threw myself. We both went over on our faces and the balloons burst. They sounded just like the gunshots going off all round.

The reply to the yammering was a big whistling, and a tremendous explosion, bright as day. I could see earth and flaming bits going up like a fountain. That was how I noticed that another Homeward Bounder had come through at the same time as us. He was standing outlined against the explosion, looking thoroughly bewildered, and he was wearing white, which made him a perfect target.

I dived up at him and grabbed him and pulled him down too. "Get down, you fool! Don't you know a war when you see one?"

I didn't have much of a sight of him, but you don't need very long to get an idea of a person. He

only looked a year or so older than I did. He looked
to be a right one, too. He was the image of all the
posh boys from the posh school—Queen Elizabeth
Academy—that we used to call names after. He had
a long fair serious face, all freckles, and nice curly
fair hair. The shape of him was posh too, if you see
what I mean. I am scraggly, with a wiry twist to the
tops of my legs. He was straight—what you call
well-knit—straight all over, including the way he
looked at me with straight serious blue eyes.

"Is this a war?" he said, as he landed beside me.
I went *chuff*, because we landed so hard. He didn't.
He was athletic. "What's going on?"

I meant to blister him. But there were definitely
tears running out of those blue eyes of his. "Oh,
don't tell me!" I said. "You're new to the Bounds! I
seem fated to run a nursery school these days!"

A terrible din prevented any of us saying
anything for a minute. Those explosions were
bursting all round, and in the yellow sky, like
gigantic fireworks. We could hear pieces of metal
from them thumping down all round us. I really
quite pitied this boy if it was his first time through a
Boundary. Baptism of fire, as they say.

After a bit, when things grew quieter, I said,
"This has happened to me quite often by now.
That's the trouble with Boundaries. Lots of them
are in empty land, and empty land makes a lovely
place for two armies to fight. What's happened is
that we seem to have arrived between two armies

who are having a war. The thing that matters to us, is how big this war is. Look out for soldiers. If they're all wearing bright colors, it's quite a small war, and we'll have a chance to slip out between them. It's when they're wearing mud-color that you're in trouble. Mud-color wars go on for miles."

Helen pointed to the left. A bunch of soldiers was chasing across between bushes there. They carried long guns, and the yellow light showed everything about them to be the dreariest mud-brown color.

"Thanks, Helen," I said. "A real pal, you are. Well, we know the worst now. We'd better find somewhere we can hide up till morning."

"We could do worse than make for those bushes," suggested our new boy.

"And go now, while we can still see," said Helen.

"Yes," I said. He was competent too, just like Helen. Blast them both! "What's your name, by the way?"

"Joris," he said, and he sort of half sat up as he said it, making a bow. I saw he had some kind of black sign painted on the front of his white clothes. It was just like the Homeward Bounder signs, but it wasn't any I knew. That made two I didn't know. I didn't like it. I was beginning to feel ignorant.

"Get down!" I said. "You're in white. You'll get shot at. We're all going to have to wriggle on our faces for a while. My name's Jamie. She's Helen

Haras-uquara and I'm her native guide. Get wriggling, Helen."

We got wriggling. Helen was practically invisible with her hair over her face. My red clothes didn't show up much in that light either, but I was worried about Joris in white. I kept turning round to look. But he was doing better than I was. He might not be used to wars, but he was used to keeping out of sight. I kept taking him for a stone.

I don't like competent posh people, I thought.

About then, a huge machine came grinding up from somewhere and ran over half the bushes and the soldiers we had seen. Joris looked pretty sick at that, but I don't suppose I looked very happy myself. Wars are beastly things.

Gunfire started crashing again as we reached what was left of the bushes. Helen and I froze. But Joris really was competent. He wriggled on and found a soldiers' hideout hidden under the bushes. It was a fairly deep hole in the ground with a tin roof and earth piled on the tin. There was some more tin and some sacking to shut the entrance with. And inside were sacks stuffed with sand and a lamp of some sort on a sack in the middle.

"This is great!" I said. I gushed a bit, to make Joris feel wanted. He showed us the hole with such a nervous air, as if he was sure experienced Homeward Bounders like us would expect something better. "Let's get that doorway blocked. Then we can light that lamp and live in real comfort."

Helen did expect something better. "What do you call *dis*comfort then?" she said as she climbed in. "It smells. And what do we light the lamp with?"

That stumped me, I must confess. "Oh, as to that," Joris said. He felt behind the part of his clothes which had the sign painted on it. "I have a lighter here. If you would make sure the door is blocked first. I think someone might shoot at a light."

Helen and I blocked the entrance while Joris clicked away with his lighter-thing, and shortly the lamp was burning cosily. I took a look round the hole, hoping for food, but we were out of luck there. "No food," I said, sitting down on a sandbag.

Joris said, "Oh, as to that," again, and felt in the front of those clothes of his. I looked at his getup with interest, now I could see it properly. It seemed to be as much of a uniform as the mud-color of the soldiers. The white stuff had baggy sleeves and baggy trousers, and it was some strange thick material which showed not a mark from all that wriggling on the ground. He had long white boots on his feet. And the part where the black sign was painted was white leather, like a tough leather pullover. From behind this part, Joris took his hand out with three blocks of chocolate in it. "This isn't much, but it's something," he said.

"You travel well-prepared," Helen said. "Light and food."

Joris was looking at her with the same kind of amazement that I had when I first saw Helen. All he could see of her was a sheet of black hair and the tip of a nose. He nodded to the nose politely. "I'm a demon hunter," he said, as if that explained everything.

There followed another crashing of guns. It was so near that I got up and made sure the door wasn't showing a light. Joris winced at the noise.

"Are wars very common?" he asked me.

"About every sixth world," I said. "Sometimes I think war is *Their* favorite thing to play. Half the other worlds are either just working up to a war or just finished one."

Joris nodded. His straight face was very straight. "Oh," he said. *"Them."* The way he said it proved he really was new to the Bounds. It was fresh new hatred, like Helen's, not weary old hatred, like mine.

We sucked our sherbert sweets and we ate Joris's chocolate, in nibbles to make it last, and listened to the guns crashing. Joris amused me, the way he kept glancing at the bits of Helen's face that showed when she parted her hair to eat, then looking away as if he was afraid, like I had been, that her face was sacred.

"It's all right," I said. "Her face isn't sacred. She's just peculiar."

Helen put one side of her hair behind an ear in order to glower at me, and jerked her head at the noise overhead. "Are we going to get *any* peace tonight?"

"Shouldn't think so," I said. "Mud-browners never seem to sleep. They always fight all night."

"In that case," Helen said, hooking the other side of her hair up and turning the whole fierce pointed sacredness at Joris, "we'd better talk. Tell us who you are and what you did to make *Them* exile you. Then we'll tell you about us."

I tried telling Helen that you didn't ask Homeward Bounders about themselves, or talk about *Them*. But she just looked contemptuous. And Joris looked anxiously from one to the other of us, wondering which was right. "Oh, go ahead," I said, "if you want to talk. Don't mind me. I've only been on a hundred worlds to her three." At that, Joris looked as if he wanted to talk but didn't know how to start. So I said, to get him going, "I can see you're new to the Bounds. You come from somewhere where they speak English too, don't you?"

He hesitated a moment, then said, "Well, as a matter of fact, I was born in Cardsburg, and I can still speak Kathayack a little. But I was sold to the Khans when I was seven, and I've spoken English ever since—"

"You were what?" I said.

"Sold," he said, looking slightly surprised. "I'm a slave, you know. Doesn't it show?"

"How could it show?" I said. "You're pulling my leg." Or so much for my ideas about posh boys, I thought.

His freckled face went quite pink with worry. "It

should appear in my manner. I hope I've not grown presumptuous."

It just shows you. You wander every kind of world, and you still get surprised like this. Helen didn't believe him either. "Prove you're a slave," she said.

"Of course," Joris said, very humbly, and began rolling up his right sleeve. This felt familiar. I began to wonder what Joris's arm was going to turn into. But it was an ordinary freckled white arm, with a good many more muscles than mine, and at the top, near the shoulder, there was—well, it looked like a little blurred pink drawing. A drawing of an anchor.

One look, and I leaped off my sandbag. "Where did you get that?"

"It's Konstam's mark," Joris said. His eyes filled with tears. "I'm Konstam's personal slave, you see. Konstam bought me."

Little did I know how soon I would be groaning at the sound of that name! At the time, as I looked at that anchor, it seemed like an omen, a sign, a lucky charm. I swore to myself as I sat down again that I'd hang on to Joris too next time the Bounds called. Meanwhile, Helen was leaning forward giving the arm and the mark the full fierce boot-button treatment. "Anyone can have themselves tattooed," she said.

Joris wiped his tears with a finger and said, almost proudly, "It isn't a tattoo. It's a brand. They do it with a hot iron."

"How disgusting!" Helen said. I liked that from her. I told you the kind of world she came from.

"They give you an injection first," Joris said. I could tell he was used to explaining to worried ladies. "It doesn't hurt."

It may not have hurt him, but it worried me. I fell to thinking about *Them*, and whether it was *Them* who did this kind of thing to people, or whether people did it to themselves. But I didn't have much space to think, because, now Joris had got going, he got going with a vengeance.

"Konstam chose me, out of all the slaves in the mart," he said, "to train as his assistant. He took me back to Khan Valley and he gave me a really good education. I mean, it's not necessary to do more than read and write in order to train as a demon hunter, you know, but Konstam's never given me anything but the best possible treatment. Konstam's really marvelous. He's the best demon hunter working today. You know, Konstam can sense a demon when none of the instruments give even a corporeal reading, I swear it. And Konstam's great company too. He never treats me like a slave. From the way he treats me, people think I'm his free-born assistant, just like you did. But I never presume on it. I try to do everything Konstam wants. I honestly tried today, but I let him down dreadfully."

Actually, I've cut down on the Konstams, telling this. Konstam came in every other word. Long before Joris had got to this point, Helen and I had got the idea: Konstam was a Great God. He was ten foot tall, dark, handsome, strong, skillful, kind, considerate—you name a virtue, Konstam had it. He was rich too—demon hunting seemed to pay well. According to Joris, Konstam drove an expensive fast car and stayed in the best hotels, and insisted on the best of everything. He lavished the best of everything on Joris too. I suppose this meant that Joris was a good slave, since he must have been one of the expensive things Konstam insisted on. Well—I'd heard of slavish devotion, but I'd never met it before.

"How much were you worth as a slave?" I asked, to divert Joris from Konstam-worship a bit.

"Oh, about twenty-thousand crowns," Joris said seriously. "I'd be worth at least twice as much if I was fully trained. But—I suppose I never will be now. I've let Konstam down—"

Helen shot me a nasty look. She always did if I talked about how much things were worth. She said I was commercial-minded. "Tell about demons," she said. "How do you hunt them?"

"Demons," said Joris. "They're quite hard to explain if you've never seen one."

Neither of us had. Demons must have been the one nasty thing that Helen's world didn't have.

"I think," said Joris, "that demons are the war that *They* play in my world. Demons hate humans. They really are utterly malignant. We have to keep them from spreading, because they can kill people outright; or they can enter into people and possess them—you know, work them like puppets; or they can haunt a place and poison it for living in; or they can drain off a person's mind, so that the person can be walking about, while his mind is elsewhere in agonies. They can do all sorts of other things too. They really are dangerous, and they're not made like us humans at all. We're half body and half soul. Demons are never that corporeal—they have more spirit than body, always. If you're trained to look for it, you can see the spirit as well as the body. Demon spirit is more visible than human—much more."

"Then what do demons look like?" we asked.

"It's hard to describe," said Joris, "to someone who's never seen one. They can change their shapes, you see. But basically, the most corporeal ones are the most grotesque, with lots of arms and legs— horrible—and red and gray and blue. Some of the more spiritual ones look like long white humans, but they usually have at least one extra pair of arms."

"How do you hunt for them?" said Helen.

"That's rather technical," said Joris. "Basically, you have to find their lair and then tempt them out of it. Or, if they won't come out, you have to go in and get them. Konstam's wonderfully brave and cool at that. There are all sorts of ways of killing them, but however you do it, you always have to kill them twice—once for the body and once for the spirit. If you don't, they grow back again—and they usually come after you when they have. In order to kill them spiritually, of course, you have to go into the spirit world. Konstam always does that. He's taught me how to, but he says it's too dangerous for me yet. I— I wire the demons for him—only—only I let him down over that today."

Joris gulped and shed tears here. It took him a while to get going again. It really had been only that day, it turned out, that he had been made a Homeward Bounder for going after a demon too hard.

That morning, Joris and Konstam had been called out to investigate a case of demon-infestation at a remote farm. It was nothing very bad, the farm people said. They had found a sheep with all the blood sucked out of it, and no animals would go near the old barn up the hill. But the demon hadn't shown itself or tried to harm the humans, which made them think it could only be a small one. Konstam had warned Joris to be careful, though. When a demon hides up and starts sucking blood, that means it's thinking of having a brood of baby demons. It gets very vicious then.

Anyway, they went to the barn and took readings and, sure enough, it seemed to be a small demon. So they set to work to tempt it out. Now, it all got very technical here, but, as far as I could gather, Joris's main job, as soon as the demon came out, was to stop it escaping into the spirit world so that Konstam could get a shot at it and kill the part of it that passed for its body—the corporeal part.

They used stuff called demon wire for that.

Here Joris broke off and got all unhappy again. He kept tapping the sign on his chest and saying, "But I *can't* be taken to the spirit world! I carry all sorts of equipment to stop it. Konstam insists. I don't know *what* happened!"

"Do you mean that sign should stop you?" said Helen.

"That?" said Joris. "No that's Shen. That's just power over demons. No, I have all sorts of other things. Anyway—"

Well, the demon came charging out, and it seemed pretty small. Joris did his stuff, while Konstam stood ready to shoot, and he did it well and got a loop of his wire round the demon. Then all hell broke loose. Because the demon had been cunningly concealing its size. It wasn't a small one at all. It was one of the long white human-looking kind, only one of the very biggest, the kind they call Great Demons, a sort of Demon King, really. Its name was Adrac, and it was almost all spirit. The body part of it was so small that Konstam missed it with his first shot, and all his other shots went wide, because the demon was dragging Joris hither and yon and trying to put Joris in the way of Konstam's bullets. They have to be silver bullets, Joris said. But any bullet kills a human, and Konstam obviously didn't want to shoot a valuable slave. So Konstam dropped his gun and came after Adrac with his demon knife. Joris said that was very brave of Konstam.

As for what happened next, Joris didn't tell it quite like this, but my guess is that his slavish devotion took over. He had been told by the Great God Konstam never, on any account, to let go of a demon once he had it wired, and he didn't. He hung on. Konstam seems to have had more sense. The last thing Joris heard of him, Konstam was shouting to him to let go. But it was too late then. The demon took Joris into another world.

"What? Through a Boundary, you mean?" I said.

"Oh no," said Joris. "We keep the Boundaries sealed off or the demons would be infesting every world by now. But there are an awful lot of weak places where a strong demon can burst through into another world. We use the weak places ourselves sometimes, to go after escaped demons."

Helen and I were both quite dumbfounded by this. We had thought no one but Homeward Bounders went from world to world. But, it turned out, Joris had actually been on quite a number of other worlds himself. With Great God Konstam, of course.

"I wonder *They* allow you to," Helen said.

Joris looked as if he was going to say it would take more than *Them* to stop Konstam, but maybe he had doubts about that, because he said, "Well, I think *They* like to keep the game between humans and demons as even as possible, and it wouldn't be even if we couldn't go after them."

On this occasion, Adrac didn't stop when he had dragged Joris into the next world. He (or it) went on, from one world to another, and Joris hung on, with worlds flipping past him like sleepers under a railway train, long after most people with any sense would have let go. Adrac kept turning round and saying, "Why don't you let go?" and Joris kept saying, "No, I'm damned if I shall!" And Adrac said, "I shall suck your blood. I'll take your mind away!" And Joris said, "You can't, not with this wire." So Adrac said, "We'll take a plunge into the spirit world then, and you'll be at my mercy there." I can't think why Joris wasn't scared silly. But he said he wasn't scared, not then, because he knew Adrac couldn't do any of those things. Konstam's equipment was too good. So the demon went on scudding from world to world, and Joris went on hanging on. He unhooked the white gauntlets from his belt to show us how the wire had almost cut through them. His hands were still sore, he said.

Finally Adrac got quite exasperated. "I'll give you one last chance," he said. "Will you let go, or shall I see what *They* can do to you?"

And Joris said, "No." He had never heard of *Them*. He thought it was another empty threat.

Adrac said, "Right, then!" And, Joris said, the demon seemed to change direction and plunge off a new way, from world to world, until suddenly they crashed into quite a different place. Joris could tell it was different from the worlds they had been racing through up to then. For one thing, it hurt Joris to crash through into it. He yelled with pain, and Adrac turned and gave a nasty laugh. For another thing, though the place felt more intense and solid than anywhere he had ever been, Joris couldn't see it very well. It was a vast, quiet, shadowy place. Machines hummed and flickered there. And *They* were there, at *Their* gaming tables.

There was a table every few yards, Joris said, for further than he could see on all sides of him. *They* bent over the tables. He saw *Them* consult machines, and then carefully move pieces this way and that on the tables, and then sometimes *They* shook dice and consulted over that. Some played in pairs, others in companies. It was all very intent. Part of the horror was the terrible intentness of *Them*.

The intensity and the sheer numbers of *Them* shook Joris to the core. And the nature of *Their* game. The nearest table he could see was his own world. *They* were moving humans and demons about in it. But, an instant or so after Adrac had come crashing in beside the table with Joris, a blue light began blinking at one end of the table, and *They* turned round to look.

Joris said he was scared stiff then. "I think it *must* have been the spirit world, in spite of my equipment," he said. "It felt so different. And I hadn't any protection with me against the spirit world at all, because Konstam always did that part. I knew I was done for. There were so many of *Them*, and I could see *They* were all demons."

"All demons?" Helen and I said together.

"Oh yes." Joris was surprised we hadn't known. "*They*'re not any kind I've ever seen before, but *They* certainly are demons. *They*'re more corporeal than Adrac, and a good deal larger, and the strongest I've ever come across, but there was no mistaking it. I could see *Their* spirit part shimmering round *Them*. And I was really frightened."

Adrac seemed fairly subdued too. He and Joris both stood there waiting, until, one by one, each table of *Them* turned *Their* hard-to-see faces to look at the two. When *They* were all looking, one in the distance said, "What are you doing here, Adrac?"

"I've come to complain," said Adrac. "You haven't kept your promises."

Another of *Them*, a nearer one, said, "Mind your manners, Adrac. Speak to us like that again, and you'll be punished."

Adrac said, in a mutinous, polite way, "Well, is it fair? We Great Demons agreed to play, if you promised not to let the humans cull among us. You agreed they could catch the small fry, and you promised we'd be allowed to breed in peace. You said you'd keep them off. I go to a quiet farm to start a family and— Well, look at me! Look at *it*!"

The hard-to-see faces turned to Joris.

"How did this happen?" one of *Them* in the distance asked *Them* at the table of Joris's world.

They looked over *Their* table, consulted a machine,

and looked carefully at the table again. One of *Them* turned to Adrac. "We apologize, Adrac. This seems to be a random factor we didn't notice."

"Well, kill it for me then," said Adrac.

"Can't you?" said one of *Them*.

"I wish I could," said Adrac. "But look at it. It's hung about with every kind of protection. I can't touch it, even here. You'll have to do it."

They started moving towards Joris then, numbers of *Them*, tall and vague and gray. Joris said he dropped the demon wire in sheer terror and hardly knew what happened the next few seconds, he was so frightened. It was only when *They* stopped, in a ring round him, that he noticed he was still alive and untouched, with his demon knife in his hand.

"Leave me alone," he said. "I was only doing my duty."

They didn't seem to notice that he'd spoken. "No good," said one.

"Why were they allowed this much protection?" asked another.

"I said all along that it was a mistake," Adrac said righteously.

They ignored Adrac too. Joris said it was the queerest feeling to find Adrac, one of his world's Great Demons, treated as a nobody. He would have enjoyed it, if he hadn't been less than nobody himself.

"This is a nuisance," said another of *Them*. "You'll have to make a discard instead."

"Have the Bounds room for any more?" asked another one.

A voice of *Them* in the distance said, "There is room for two more discards only. Can't it really be touched?"

"No it can't!" one of *Them* round Joris said, quite irritably. "The only solution is a discard."

"Well get on and discard then," said another of *Them* in the distance. "You're holding up play."

So the nearest of *Them* turned to Joris and said just what *They* said to me. "You are now a discard. We have no further use for you in play. You are free to walk the Bounds as you please, except that it is against the rules for you to enter play in any world. To ensure that you keep this rule, you will be transferred to another field of play every time a move ends in the field where you are. The rules also state that you are allowed to return Home if you can. If you succeed in returning, you may enter play again in the normal manner."

Adrac laughed meanly, and Joris found himself a Homeward Bounder. The next thing he knew, he was in the middle of the war.

VIII

Helen had spent the time collecting critters. She had about twenty woodlice in front of her on the sack, and she was arranging them into an armor-plated pattern. "Never mind," she said. "At least you're not a slave any longer."

Joris burst into tears. "You don't understand! I belong to Konstam!"

"Stop howling," said Helen, "or you won't hear me when I tell you what happened to me. Or Jamie, when he tells."

"I don't think we should," I said. "I was told it was against the rules."

Helen sighed angrily. "There are no rules. There are only principles and—"

"I know, I know!" I said. "But I broke a rule once."

"Well, *They* don't seem to have eaten you," said Helen. "*They* probably don't care. To *Them*, we're only discarded randoms, and children too. When I was born, Joris, I was born with a gift."

I dozed off while Helen told it. The guns outside

were still crumping and yattering, but you get used to them, and then they make you feel tired. But I remember noticing that Helen played down her peculiar arm when she told it to Joris. She kept calling it just her gift. Then she woke me up and made me tell Joris what had happened to me, while she paid me back by going to sleep over the sack, with her face in the woodlice. After that, Joris told me a great deal more about ten-foot Konstam's godlike virtues, and I went to sleep again too. I think we were all three asleep when a mud-brown officer came hammering on our metal roof.

"Put that light out, you in there! The dawn offensive is due to start any moment now!"

I suppose it was typical of each of us, the way we took that. Joris jumped up before he was really awake and obediently blew out the light. I woke up and growled out, "Very good, sir. Sorry, sir," in a voice I hoped sounded like a soldier's. Helen did nothing but wake up and glower.

"Don't let it occur again," said the officer. And he went away without looking inside, to our relief.

We sat in the dark and listened to the din. It was offensive all right. If the officer hadn't woken us, the noise would have done. Our ears hurt with it. The earth in our hole quivered. It sounded as if all the guns outside were firing at once, nonstop. Feet ran across our roof quite often, adding to the din, and once I think one of the machines ran over it too. It certainly sounded like it from underneath. At last, when we could see chinks of quite bright daylight round the sacking, the noise all moved away into the distance. It was most peaceful. We actually heard a bird sing.

Helen said, "I *hate* this world! How long have we got to be here?"

"Quite a while," I said glumly. "It feels like a couple of months."

"Why's that?" said Joris.

I explained to him about the Bounds calling whenever one of *Them* playing the world you were in finished a move, and how you always knew roughly when it was due.

"Yes, I realize," he said. "That's how *They* transfer us to stop us entering play. But we can surely go back to the Boundary now and try for a better world if we want."

"Can we?" I said. I didn't think it was possible.

"Why not?" asked Helen. "We don't have to keep *Their* rules."

"No—" said Joris. "I meant I don't think it *is* a rule. *They* didn't tell me I couldn't use the Boundaries any time I wanted. *They* said 'You are free to walk the Bounds' as if I *could*. We can use Boundaries any time in my world."

"Provided you approach along a Bound, I suppose," said Helen. "Yes, why not? That's the nature of a traverse."

Really, Helen and Joris knew so much about the Bounds that they made me feel quite ignorant. "But how do we know which is a Bound without the call?" I objected. "This Boundary wasn't marked at all."

"Oh, as to that," Joris said—he always said that when he was about to produce something from under his white leather jerkin—"as to that, I've got an instrument here that will tell us."

"What about bringing out a white rabbit or so, while you're at it?" I said. It was meant to sound grumpy, but I'm not sure that it did. All of a sudden, hope was roaring in my ears. If this was true, I could go anywhere I wanted. I could zip across world after world, like Joris's demon, and end up at Home. Now. Soon. Today!

Joris saw the joke and laughed. That was the trouble with Joris. He was nice. You ended up liking him, whatever you did. Even when you wanted to shake him till his head fell off.

We set off at once, before the war could come back. When we scrambled out of the hole, blinking, there seemed to be nothing anywhere but mud and litter. The bushes had gone, and most of the grass. It was all wheeltracks and raw holes and things thrown about. One of the thrown things was a half-opened mud-brown bag with packets of soldiers' rations tumbling out of it. I scooped that up while Joris was casting about with his little clocklike instrument to find the line of the Bound. After that, I hung on to Joris's baggy white sleeve, and Helen hung on to my red one. We didn't want to lose one another.

"Found it!" said Joris. The needle on his little clock swung and quivered. We walked where it pointed, in a cluster, treading on one another's heels, until we came to a muddy place that looked no different from the rest of the battlefield, where the needle began to swirl round and round. "Boundary," said Joris. We stumbled on a step or so.

There is not even a twitch if you do it of your own free will. You are just there. And it was lucky it happened to be raining in that next world. Otherwise we wouldn't have noticed the difference. It was another battlefield, just the same, mud, wheel-tracks, litter and all. I picked up another bag of food there, but it was pretty soggy. Guns clapped away in the distance.

"I'm not staying here," Helen said.

It took us a whole hour to find a reasonable world, where we could even sit down and eat. Most of that time was taken up with walking out into war-spoilt countrysides in order to find the Bound line, so that we could move on again. For, as Joris explained to me, not being demons, we couldn't go straight from world to world. The Boundaries would only work for us if we came to them along the Bounds. So we had to trudge off into each desolate landscape we came to, until Joris's instrument told us we had come to a Bound. Then we followed it back to the Boundary and moved on.

We seemed to have hit a kind of war-sequence.

There were about eight worlds, and every single one of them had obviously just had a war. We thought the *Them* playing them must have had a competition to see which could produce the nastiest war. I was going to give the prize to the *Them* responsible for the ruined city we found about fifth world along. It had only been done about a week before, and there were still corpses. But that was before we came to the eighth world. That took the prize. It was a desert—a desert made of bits of broken brick and ash, mostly, with every so often a place where other things had been melted into sort of glassy smears, with trickles at the edges. There didn't seem to be a thing alive there.

As soon as we got there, Joris's clock-thing began to click. It sounded like someone saying "Tut-tut, tut-tut." I thought it had the right idea. Joris jumped at the sound and turned the clock over. Another needle was flicking there, a flick to every *tut*. Joris hurriedly compared it with another clock-thing he wore on his wrist. "I don't like this," he said. "This place is full of demon beams, but there aren't any demons."

Helen hooked her hair behind her ears to look first at the tut-tutting needle, then at the spread of crumbled brick and glassy smears. She knew about it. I told you the kind of world she came from. "We call them death rays," she said. "Or radiation. You can make them with weapons. We must get out of here quick. How bad is it?"

"Quite bad," said Joris. "We can only take about five minutes."

We raced round in a circle, stumbling and crunching in the rubble, frantic to find the Bound. It only took us half a minute, but it seemed hours. As we crunched along in a line, all hanging on to one another, Joris panted out that these beams or rays or whatever gave ordinary people a nasty lingering death. Being Homeward Bounders, we'd have been lingering for a mighty long time. I was really scared.

That was the only world in which Joris didn't talk about Konstam all the time. As soon as we got to the next world, he began again. "Konstam never lets me go near any demon beams. He makes me go back and wait as soon as they register. I'd no idea you didn't feel anything. Konstam didn't tell me."

I had stopped listening by then. As soon as I heard the word *Konstam*, I switched my ears off. I heard Helen's answer. "No, you don't feel a thing. They just go through you. The Hands of Uquar thought my gift might be due to them." Then Joris was on about Konstam again, and my ears were off.

I stood and had a private shudder. This world we were in now was green and almost natural. There were buzzings and hummings and chirpings, and some deep droning in the distance. A white butterfly flittered by in front of my face. It wasn't the cleanest air I'd ever breathed, but I took deep breaths of it. I was fairly sure it wasn't lethal. And I realized that the worst thing about that desert world had been the silence. The complete, dead silence. You never get silence like that in a world where anything lives.

I took a look around. It was a nice warm day in this world, with a pale blue sky and fluffy white clouds about in it. We were in a big field full of little separate vegetable gardens. Each garden grew the same sort of things, over and over, in a different order, so that wherever you looked you saw rows of big bluish cabbages, sets of sticks covered with red bean-flowers and piercing green lines of lettuces. Every garden had a messy little hut at one end of it. At first I thought it must be a very poor world if people lived in that kind of hut, but when I looked closely, I saw the huts were all empty. There didn't seem to be a soul about in the gardens.

"We can sit down and have a bite to eat here," I said. I was interrupting what Joris was saying about Konstam, but if you didn't do that you never got to talk at all. Helen and I interrupted Joris all the time by then.

"I'd like a lettuce," Helen said.

"Yes, and I can see radishes," I said.

It wasn't quite fair, I suppose. But we both knew by then that, because of being a slave, Joris would think it his duty to go off and pinch people's vegetables for us. And he did. Helen and I sat on a patch of grass by one of the huts, sorting out the good food in my mud-brown bags from the packets that were soggy or trodden-on, and watched Joris, clean and white and dutiful, searching along the earthy rows and diligently pulling up radishes.

"I suppose he'll notice he's not a slave any longer in the end," I said.

"Not for a hundred years, at the rate he's going," Helen said. "If he talks about ten-foot-tall Konstam much more, I shall bite him. I shan't be able to help it."

"It's not just the talk," I said. "It's the way Konstam can do no ill that gets up my nose. It can't be true. Nobody could be that tall, that brave, that strong, that considerate and all the rest of it!" While I said that, a picture came into my head, of him chained to his rock. He *was* pretty well ten foot tall, and I rather thought he was most of the other things Joris said Konstam was as well. I wished I hadn't thought of him. It upset me every time I did.

"Ah, but you see," Helen said, "Konstam is the Great God."

"I once met—" I began. But Joris came dutifully back just then, looking as though, if he'd had a tail, he'd have been wagging it. He had a handsome hearty lettuce, a bundle of spring onions, radishes, and some little pink carrots. So, once again, I didn't tell Helen about him on his rock. And lucky I didn't. "Those look good!" I said to Joris. You felt he needed praising like a dog. Joris beamed when I said it, and that annoyed me into saying meanly, "Nothing but the best for the young master and mistress, eh?"

A very hurt, pale, freckly look came over Joris's face. He laid the vegetables carefully down by the other food and said, "I'm not your slave. I'm Konstam's."

"I know that, you fool!" I said. I felt terrible. "Can't you get it through your head that you're not even that any longer?"

"Yes," said Joris.

"Then—" I said.

"But I've made up my mind never to forget all Konstam did for me," said Joris.

What can you say to that? I tried to make up for it while we were eating by listening to Joris talking about Konstam, instead of shutting my ears down. It seemed the least I could do. Helen shut her hair down and collected caterpillars. I don't think she listened. Joris was on about Konstam's family now, the Khans.

The Khans were a huge family—clan, more like—and they were all devoted to demon hunting in one way or another. They were so rich that they owned an entire big valley with farms, factories, an airfield, schools and libraries, all run by Khans, for Khans. They made all the equipment Joris carried, and more, in that valley. They were very machine-minded, the Khans, far more than my Home and even more than Helen's. They owned a lot of flying machines so that the demon hunters could get to the demons quickly. While Joris talked, a silver flying machine went booming over our heads in that world, and I asked him if the Khans' fliers were the same. I love fliers. I've always wanted to go in one. Joris glanced up at it—his mind was miles away, in his own world—and said no, his were rather different. And he went straight on to how only the best of the Khans actually hunted demons. The others stayed in the valley and invented new and better equipment.

I think the Khans were pretty good to Joris. They don't seem to have treated him like a slave. And I think this was true, because Joris didn't say it. With Joris, you always had to notice the things he *didn't* say. In the same way, I got the idea that Konstam probably *did* treat Joris like a slave. The Chief Khan seems to have been pretty angry with Konstam for buying Joris. She didn't hold with slaves. The Chief Khan was a lady. It must have been about the only thing Joris's Khans had in common with my first cattle people—they had a Mrs. Chief. This Mrs. Chief was called Elsa Khan and Joris was terrified of her. It took me a while to sort out about her, though, because there was another Elsa Khan too, who was the same age as Joris—I think she was the Chief Khan's granddaughter. Joris thought the world of this small Elsa. He didn't say so of course, but it was obvious. In the most respectful possible way, naturally.

It was over these Elsas that I began to see why Joris's talk made me not want to listen. My sister's name was Elsie. Elsie was nothing like Elsa Khan. Elsie had ginger hair. According to Joris, his Elsa had black hair and brown skin, like Helen's. He said several times, respectfully, that Helen looked like a

Khan. Helen said nothing and went on collecting caterpillars. I said nothing, but the cold foot ache grew inside me. It was just the name. But before long, Joris had only to mention the name Khan, or Konstam, to make me feel really sick inside for Home.

I was quite glad when Helen interrupted Joris. "That last world with the rays," she said. "Do you think *They* killed off all the people because *They*'d got tired of playing?"

"No," I said. "*They*'ll have left a few to start a new game with. I've been on a world where *They* were just starting again after a flood."

"I hate *Them*," Helen said.

"Yes, but don't go on about it," I said, and I got up. Joris had set Helen off too, I could tell. Her version of my cold foot was vicious hate of *Them*. It seemed to be best to get moving to take all our minds off Home.

Down the road from the vegetables there was a smallish town. The moment we set foot in its main street, I could tell this was going to be a difficult world for Homeward Bounders. It had all the signs. In some worlds, you can say you come from the next town and people believe you. Not in this one. There were wires overhead so that they could talk to the next town and ask if you did. The houses were orderly and well painted. The streets were clean. The people kept to the sidewalks and machines ran politely up and down the road. All was law and order. And people stared at us.

"Why are they staring?" Joris said nervously. "Will they arrest us?"

I suppose we did look odd. Helen would look odd in any world. Nobody was wearing red all over like me. And Joris struck even me as outlandish, all in white, with that black sign painted on his chest.

"No one bothers about what children wear," I said airily. I said it to calm Joris. He was new to the Bounds, after all.

The words were hardly out of my mouth, when a woman stopped us. "Do tell me, dears. Red and white and black. What are you? Are you collecting for something, or is it a pageant at school?"

"A pageant," I said promptly. "He's a demon hunter and we two are the demons." Helen's reaction to this was to put her caterpillar collection, gently and secretly, into the woman's shopping basket. I thought it was a revenge on me, but it was for the woman. Helen's revenge on me came a minute or so later. "We must go," I said hastily. "We have to be on the stage in five minutes." And I hurried us away into a side street before the woman could get round to looking in her basket. "Don't *do* things like that!" I said to Helen.

Helen took even her nose inside her hair. She stood there with no face and said one word. "Cannibals."

"Who are?" Joris said, alarmed. There was a butcher's shop across the way, and he looked at it rather narrowly. It said Family Butcher over the window.

I didn't think this was like the cannibal world, and I knew Helen didn't. "It's all right," I said to Joris. "She just means she thinks I'm showing off. Honestly, Helen, you haven't given me a chance! I was going to tell you—this looks to be a really difficult world. I can see they have strict laws. Children are supposed to be at school. They bother about clothes. It may be one of those worlds where you have to have papers to show all the time, and we could be in real trouble. What do you say, both of you? Shall we go back to the veg and try the next world?"

If I'd known how much hung on their decision, I'd have been chewing my nails and jumping up and down on the pavement. As it was, I assumed they'd agree with me and set off up the street.

Before I'd got very far, Helen shouted, "Come back!" And when I did, she said, "This is the first decent world since Creema di Leema, *and* they speak a language we all know."

And when I looked at Joris, he said seriously, "I think I'd like to see what the difficulties are. If we ever get separated, I'd be glad of the experience."

"Two to one," said Helen.

"All right," I said. "But don't blame me if we get put in prison, and Rule Two starts killing judges and policemen all round us."

"What do we do now?" Helen said. It was her

stony manner, the one you couldn't argue with.

"Make for a city," I said, "if there is one. Nobody knows anyone in a city, and you get away with more lies there."

I led the way on up that street in order not to run into the woman with the caterpillars again. Helen and Joris lagged a bit, so I turned round to see why. And there was Joris grinning at Helen, and Helen parting her hair in order to smirk back. I was furious. They were taking the Archangel—as they say in some worlds. This was Helen's revenge. She and Joris thought I showed off about all my experience, so they'd chosen to stay here to see what kind of mess I got them into.

All *right*! I thought. I'll show them!

As I turned round again, there was a train going across a bridge over the street. I love trains, even more than I love flying machines. I used to love the trains at Home. This was nothing like those trains. It was flat both ends and a clean bright blue—but it was still a train. I thought, I'll show those two how to get a ride on a train, and set off to find the station.

The railway station was just round the corner. That was no good to us, because we hadn't made any money yet—if we ever could in this world—but I have never known the station where there wasn't a gate they used for parcels and things. This one had a nice wide one. I stood just outside it and spied out the land. There were railway lines and two platforms. On the platform across the way, right at the end of it, sitting on a sort of wagon, I saw a set of boys. Some of them were quite small and surely ought to have been at school, if this world was as strict as it looked. They all had notebooks and pens. Perhaps their school had sent them to study trains.

I turned to Joris. "You know," I said, "if only we had papers and pens, we could go on to the platform and pretend we were studying trains like they are." I said it on purpose, hoping Joris would do another white-rabbit trick.

Sure enough, Joris said, "Oh, as to that," and felt inside his white leather jerkin. He produced a small notebook. "This is all I—Why are you laughing?"

"Never mind," I said. "Just give us a page each, and I guarantee we'll be on the next train that comes along."

It went like clockwork. We went through the gate on to the platform and sat on a bench, fluttering our pages and looking observant. A man in uniform glanced at us from time to time, but he never spoke to us. I think he thought the boy in white was giving the other boy and the girl a learned lecture on trains. He wasn't, of course. That was Joris talking about Konstam.

A train came in and stopped at the platform. While people were getting off, we got on, quickly, up the front. Nobody noticed at all. We sat in comfortable seats up at the empty end, and the train clattered off again. Joris began on Konstam again.

We sat and looked at green countryside, until the train clattered into another station. People got off and got on. Some glanced at us curiously, but nobody spoke to us.

"Why don't we get off here?" said Helen.

"Not big enough," I said. I caught them smirking again, and ground my teeth.

The train went on, and Joris went on again too, all about Konstam. This time it was how kind and understanding Konstam had been on Joris's first demon hunt. I switched my ears off. Helen's hair moved in the way that meant she was yawning. Joris talked on, glowing with enthusiasm. The train kept stopping, but Joris never stopped, not once. By the time we were beginning to come to a city, my cold foot ache was back worse than it ever had been, and I was near screaming at him to stop. But that didn't seem kind. So I looked out at rows of little pink houses, and high glass buildings with pipes at the top which squirted smoke and steam, and a sickly green river winding in and out under the train, and prayed that Joris would talk Konstam out of his system soon.

Then a guard or something came up the train calling out, "Tickets, please!"

Joris didn't stop talking, but I saw him glance at me expectantly. Among Helen's hair I could see a beady eye, also watching me. I pretended not to see.

"All tickets, please," said the guard, standing above us.

I pointed back down the train. "My mother's got our tickets. She's er—she's er—"

The guard grunted and went away to rattle at a door marked TO LET. Luckily, the train drew into another station just then.

"Here's where we get off," I said. "Quick."

IX

I do think Helen and Joris might have stopped their joke after I got us off that city station too. I did know what I was doing, and I did it pretty well. It was a newish station, built of concrete, and small enough for there to be a man asking for tickets at the door marked WAY OUT. I marched boldly up to him and said they'd taken our tickets on the train, and he let us through. When we were outside in the station yard, I turned round to suggest to Helen and Joris that I'd taken enough of the Archangel now, and to come off it.

Almost overhead, very close, a canal went marching above the houses, and above the station, on a set of huge yellow arches.

My heart seemed to stop. Then it began banging away so hard that I could hear and feel nothing else. I seemed to have lost the lower half of me and be floating. For a moment, I could have sworn I was Home. The disappointment—I can't tell you the thump the disappointment hit me with, as if I were really floating and then had fallen, when I looked round and saw that I couldn't be Home. The place was full of machines buzzing about. In my world, people walked, or used carriages. The trains were different. People's clothes were different. The buildings were different: taller than in my Home, and straight and boxlike, with lots of windows. And now I came to look at the canal arches, they were different too: not so high, and made of dirty yellow brick, in fancy patterns.

"What's the matter?" Joris said. I must have looked peculiar.

"Nothing," I said. "I reckon we ought to look for some lunch."

I said it almost without thinking. Hope was beginning to build and roar in me again. You see, you often get sets of worlds that are very much alike—like the war set we'd just come through. In these sets, the language and the landscape and the climate and the shape of the cities can be almost identical, though the actual way people live is usually different, because that depends on the *Them* playing the world. But the nearer two worlds are in a set, the more alike they are. And I had only to look about to see that the shape of this city—the canal, the railway and the roads—was the same as the one I had been born in. And that meant I was really close to Home. It could even be next world on.

But first there were Helen and Joris to look after. I had to find them some lunch, and show them how to manage in a world like this. I took them to the shops—they were where the smart part of my city had been. And things didn't go so well there. We all got confused in the traffic, and all the shops seemed to have people watching for robbers. We had no chance to get hold of food, even in a covered-over sort of market. The trouble was, we were too noticeable, one in black, one in red and one in white. We looked like counters in a game. People looked at us all the time. It was not that they didn't wear bright clothes here—they did. Some even wore black all over like Helen. But not a soul dressed all in white with a black sign on their chest, like Joris. I began to see that we really would have to find Joris something different to wear.

In the end, I told Helen and Joris—who smirked—that I would try the "lost my money" trick in the next food shop we came to. You know—you go in and you choose a kind-looking person to do it near, and you ask them behind the counter for the food you want. Then you put your hands in your pockets and discover your money's been stolen. I've worked that dozens of times. The kind person nearly always buys you at least some of the food.

This shop said LUNCH TO TAKE AWAY. I left Helen and Joris outside and went in. The LUNCH was piles of crisp round rolls with ham and lettuce in them, stacked up behind a glass wall on the counter. And the smell of them! As soon as I got in there, I was carried away with misery. They smelled just the same as the rolls we used to stock in our shop. The baker's van used to deliver them still warm at breakfast time every day except Sunday. And my mother always used to give Rob and Elsie and me two each, with cheese, to take to school for lunch. As I stood there, smelling those rolls, it was like yesterday. I could see my mother, with a piece of hair falling down over her forehead and her face all irritable, dragging the cheese-wire down through the big lump of cheese and cutting off a small lump for each of us. And Elsie would be hanging round to pounce on any bits that crumbled off. I can't tell you how miserable it made me. I just stood there, and didn't even bother to look for a kind person.

Next thing I knew, a kind lady was saying, "What's up, my duck? You *do* look mournful."

Thank goodness Helen and Joris were outside! I looked up at her, and I meant to say the piece about having lost my money. But you know what I said? I said, "I've lost my mummy!" I truly did. Just as if I were four years old!

Luckily, she didn't believe her ears. She obviously thought I was too old to say things like that. Well I was. "Lost your money, have you, my duck?" she said. "Never mind. I'll buy you a roll. Two ham rolls, please miss."

I came out of the shop with a big crusty roll and practically in tears.

"Not much between three," said Helen. "What *is* wrong with you, Jamie?"

"Nothing," I said. I shared out the roll. Then I

said, "It's bothering me the way we look. We're too noticeable. We really must get Joris something else to wear at least. Your clothes will do, Helen. I'd be all right if I had darker trousers, but Joris is the one who's urgent. Nobody here wears white all over."

I met a snag here. Once he saw that I meant it, the white, hurt look settled on Joris's face. "Oh no," he said. "This is the proper dress for a demon hunter, and I'm proud to wear it. I refuse to sneak about dressed as something else!"

"Don't be a fool," I said. "You stick out like a broken leg in it. The only way we're going to get on in this world is by looking like everyone else."

"I'm damned if I shall!" said Joris. He was really angry. I wouldn't have thought he had it in him. But I suppose he went after the demon Adrac the same way.

"Put a coat on over it then," said Helen.

"And serve you right if you swelter!" I said. I was angry too.

After a lot of arguing, Joris consented to a coat. As if it were a great favor. Then, of course, we had to find a coat. "Let's go out towards the edge of the city," I said. "You get clotheslines and washing there." That is true. But the reason I suggested it was to see just how like my Home this city was. The shortest way to the outskirts from where we were would take us through the part where my courtyard should have been in my city. I wanted to see if there was anything like it here.

There wasn't, of course. When we reached that part, it was all new yellow houses being built. Since people hadn't moved into the houses yet, there were no clotheslines and no coats, and we had to go on, further out to the edge of the city. By the middle of the afternoon, Joris and Helen were exchanging meaning smirks again. They thought this world had me beat.

Luckily, we came to a long hedge about then. I could hear the sound of children's voices from behind the hedge. In my experience, wherever there are children playing, some of them are sure to have left coats or sweaters about on the ground. I pushed through the hedge.

It was better than I'd hoped. As far as I could tell, the children were all boys about the same size as me or Joris—though that was a guess, because the boys were off in the distance playing some game. They were all dressed in white. Near the hedge, a few yards away, there was a sort of house with a wooden porch in front. Beside that was one of the big machines for riding in, square, with lots of windows. I reckoned, since white was not a usual color to wear, that the boys' ordinary clothes would be either in the house or in the machine.

"I'll stay on guard," Helen said.

Joris and I left her lurking by the machine and crept across the creaking wooden floor of the porch to look inside the house-thing. It was better and better. We were right first time. The place was hung

round with clothes, plentiful supplies of dark gray
trousers, black shoes, gray shirts and red-and-blue
striped neckwear. The top thing hanging on each
bundle of clothes was a navy-blue jacket with a
badge on the top pocket. It was only a question of
finding things to fit. A good third of the gray trousers
were about my size. I chose the best fit and got into
them.

But Joris went and had another attack of demon
hunter's pride. "People do wear white here," he said,
pointing to the distant boys. "Why can't I be playing
that game out there?"

"They change to play it," I said. "They don't
walk about dressed up for it. Take one of those
jackets. Go on."

Most of the jackets were too small for Joris. I
told you he was bigger than me. And he was so
reluctant to defile his precious uniform that he took
a long time finding the one jacket that fitted him. He
had just unhooked the biggest and put one arm in its
sleeve when real disaster struck. Three of the boys
who owned the clothes walked in.

I think they had heard us. They must have done.
By that time I was swearing a blue streak at Joris.
And they came quietly on purpose. When I looked at
their faces, I could see they had been expecting to
find people stealing their clothes. My heart sank.
They were cool, scornful, unfriendly, accusing.
Underneath that, they were very indignant indeed.
But that was underneath the scorn. That was

because these three boys really were the kind of posh boy I had taken Joris for at first, and that kind of boy keeps cool if he can. The one in front was the coolest. He was about my size and he wore glasses, glasses with thick owlish rims. The boy behind him was even bigger than Joris. I didn't see the third boy very well, because the owl-boy turned to him and snapped, "Go and get Smitty," and that boy ran away.

Which left two to two. But the odds weren't really like that, because of Rule Two.

The big one looked at Joris, frozen with one arm half inside the coat. "My blazer, I believe," he said.

"And my trousers, I think," said the owl-boy, looking at me. "Do, please, go on and help yourself to my shirt while you're at it. Red shirts are not school uniform."

"You can have the trousers back," I said. There was nothing else to do, because of Rule Two. I couldn't get them both killed just for wanting their own clothes back. Joris, seeing I meant it, took his arm out of the big boy's blazer and hung it neatly up again. The two boys stared at the demon hunter's outfit, and then, slowly, both their heads turned to look at my red Creema di Leema trousers in a heap on the floor.

"Adam," said the big one. "Who *are* these people?"

"Chessmen probably," said the owlish Adam. "Red pawn and white knight, by the look of them."

"Chessmen!" I said. "If only you knew! Let me give you the trousers back and we'll go."

"I believe they give you special clothes to wear in prison," Adam said. "I'll get them back then."

Here, heavy footsteps and light ones creaked on the wooden part outside. The third boy came in with a tall, vague, bored schoolmaster. "No, sir. That wasn't quite what I meant," the boy was saying. He sounded exasperated. "They were stealing our clothes."

The teacher gave me and Joris a vague, bored look. Then he did the same to Adam and his friend. I began to feel hopeful. This teacher didn't know any of the boys well, and he had not the least idea what was really going on. "What are you two boys doing in here?" he said to me.

"I'm afraid we came without the proper clothes, sir," I said.

"That's no reason for borrowing other people's," said the teacher, "or for skulking in here. Get out on the field, both of you. You three get out there too."

He thought Joris and I were boys at the school too. I tried not to smile. How was that for quick thinking on my part? Then I met the spectacled eye of Adam. Right! that eye seemed to say to me. You wait! And, as the big boy opened his mouth to explain, Adam kicked him on the ankle. Plainly he had done some quick thinking too.

We all went in a crowd, out of the clothes-place and across the wooden platform. The teacher was between Joris and me. He might have been bored and vague, but he was doing what he thought was his duty, and seeing that we two went out to play that game, whatever it was. All I could do was go along and hope. Rule Two really ties your hands. And I've never dared test out how much—or how little—an ordinary person can do to a Homeward Bounder before Rule Two gets him. As I said, I've been beaten, and nothing has happened; and I've been robbed and sentenced to jail, and something very much *has*.

As we went out across the field, I took a look round for Helen. There was no sign of her. She must have gone through the hedge again. I looked across at Joris. He was quite placid—amused—waiting for me to get us out of this. He didn't know I couldn't. That frightened me. I couldn't remember explaining Rule Two to him, now I thought, or if I had, Joris must have been thinking of Konstam at the time and didn't listen.

The other boys in white were coming across the field towards us, staring. They knew strangers when they saw them, even if their teacher didn't. Quite a few of them drifted away behind us as we walked. Adam was signaling to them. I heard snatches of whispers.

"I know. It would be old Smitty!"

"Right then. After that." And muffled laughter.

We got to the middle of the field where the game happened. There were two sets of three little sticks stuck in the ground some way apart, and that was all. It was the most mysterious game I ever encountered. The schoolmaster wandered away to one side. "Right. Start again from the beginning of the over," he said. Then he looked at the sky and seemed to enter a private dream. This game bored him.

Two boys approached Joris and me with derisive smiles and handed each of us a pair of large white things with buckles flapping off them. They looked like the kind of splints you might wear if you had broken both legs. But I rather thought they were to stop your legs getting broken. The other boys stood round us in a ring. "Get those pads on," one of them said. "You two are batting."

There were at least twenty boys. Joris gave me a dubious look. I gave him a helpless one. Joris shrugged, and we both buckled the splints to our legs. They were huge. When I had them on, I could only walk with both legs wide apart, as if I were wading. By this time I was hating Adam. I didn't care if Rule Two got him. What better way to stop a person running away than to buckle his legs into dirty great splints?

When we were ready, they handed us each a long wooden bat and pushed each of us in front of a set of three sticks. Most of them spread out all round. The big boy picked up a red ball from somewhere and marched off beyond Joris with it. Joris turned round to stare after him, puzzled — and then turned back as the boy broke into a gallop and charged up beside him. The boy's arm whirled. Joris stuck up one elbow, thinking he was going to be hit. But the red ball whizzed out of the boy's hand and came straight at me instead, at the other end.

I saw it coming and dodged. Lucky I did. That ball was hard as a bullet. There was a wooden clatter beside me, and all three sticks fell down.

The schoolmaster came out of his dream. "Wasn't that out?"

"Oh no, sir," said a chorus of voices. "The wicket just fell down."

They built the sticks up again, and the big boy once more did his gallop up to Joris. But Joris, this time, had decided that his part in the game must be to stop the big boy victimizing me like this. He stuck his bat into the boy's stomach as the boy whirled his arm. The ball flew up into the air. The boy sat down.

"No ball!" shouted everyone. I was glad. I thought they had lost it.

The big boy bounced up and stuck his face into Joris's. I couldn't hear what they said, but I could see it was a fairly heated argument. Other boys gathered round and joined in. Joris's voice rose out of the crowd. "I'm damned if I'm going to stand here and watch while you throw red stones at him!"

A boy came out of the crowd, grinning rather, and approached Adam. Adam was standing near me and wearing splints too, making sure I didn't sneak off. "They don't know the first thing about it!"

"I can see that," Adam said. "They'll have to learn, won't they?"

"Come along, boys," said the schoolmaster, turning from the sky again.

The ball wasn't lost. The big boy took it and threw it at me five more times. These times, Joris stood glowering at the other end and did nothing but mutter remarks at the boy. I was left quite undefended. But I managed to dodge every time but once, when the ball somehow dodged with me and hit me on the leg. I was forced to hop about, which gave the boys a great deal of pleasure.

Then everyone walked about a little. While they did, Adam looked at me with contempt. "You're supposed to hit the ball," he said, and then trudged off to stand behind Joris.

Another boy came up beside me with a sort of waddling wander, squeezing the ball in his hands as he came. Then he threw it at Joris. By now, Joris had resigned himself to just standing there. He only noticed the ball at the last minute. I think it made him angry. Anyway, he hit it. I told you Joris was athletic. There was an almighty *clop*, and the ball soared out of sight.

Immediately, everyone began shouting at us. *"Run!"*

Naturally, Joris and I both dropped our bats and ran for our lives. We both thought the ball was coming down on us. And, once we were running, we both thought we might as well go on and escape.

"No!" shouted everyone. "Come back!" Most of them ran after us. Meanwhile the ball came down and just missed the schoolmaster.

They caught us fairly quickly. I couldn't run in those splints. Joris could, but he waited for me. "Can't you let us go now?" he said, as they all came up. "You've had your fun."

"Certainly not," said Adam. "I want my trousers back—my way. Can you two arch-cretins get it into your heads that a *run* means from one set of sticks to the other? Backwards and forwards."

So we went back and did it Adam's way. I thought Joris almost enjoyed it. He said he would have enjoyed it, if he hadn't felt so contemptuous. It was so easy, compared with demon hunting. He hit the ball every time they threw it at him, whatever way they threw it. Once it went right over the hedge into the road. All I seemed to do was charge up and down when they told me to. Twice they knocked the sticks down before I panted up to them. Once I knocked them down myself when I was dodging the ball. Each time, the schoolmaster came back from the clouds and asked if that meant I was out, and each time they said I wasn't. Out, I began to realize, meant that I could take the splints off and go and stand somewhere else. But they didn't want that. I might have got away.

At last, I actually hit the ball. It was coming right for my head, and I had to hit it if I didn't want to be hurt. The ball flew off sideways and Adam caught it.

"You have now," he said, "been out in every way possible. It may be a record. Shall we stop?"

"If you want to," I said weakly.

So Adam coolly walked over and interrupted the teacher's musings. "Sir, I think it's time to go now, sir."

I looked at Joris. We both sat down on the grass and unbuckled our splints as fast as we could go. But of course, the other boys weren't wearing any. We looked up to find ourselves in a ring of white-clothed legs.

"Not thinking of going, were you?" Adam said.

We stopped thinking of going just then. We put the idea off until they would be busy changing their clothes.

Adam had thought of that. Not a single boy changed. Nearly all of them stayed milling round Joris and me as we walked across the field. A few of them dashed into the house-thing and came out laden with everyone's clothes. By this time, the rest of us were in a crowd round the vehicle, and the schoolmaster was sitting in the front of it, ready to drive it. The last boy locked the house-thing and brought the key to the master.

The master seemed puzzled. "Why are none of you changed?"

"We're all going to tea with Macready, sir," the boy said. "We can change at his house."

I didn't like the sound of this at all. They were meaning to load us on that vehicle and take us off somewhere. Even if nothing else happened, we were going to lose Helen. There was no sign of Helen.

Adam stood by the door of the vehicle. "In you get," he said to me, with a chilly smile.

I dived sideways and tried to run. They had been expecting that. Four of them caught me as I dived. "No fighting now!" said the teacher from inside.

"It's all right, sir," said someone. He hauled my arm up my back and twisted it. "He just fell over." A knee went into my back and pushed me up the steps into the vehicle. Nothing happened to anyone. Rule Two didn't seem to be working, much as I wished it would. Perhaps it didn't work because Joris got into the vehicle behind me without giving any trouble at all.

There were lots of seats inside. Boys pushed past us and spread out into the seats. As they did so, Helen stood up from between two seats at the back. She had made one of her mistakes again. She had thought the vehicle was the safest place to hide in.

You get quite a shock when you first see Helen. It's the way she doesn't seem to have a face. The boy nearest her went *"Aah!"* and backed away. He was really scared, but he tried to make a joke of it. "They've landed! There's a faceless wonder here!"

"Ah," said Adam, looking over my shoulder. "The female of the species."

"What's going on *now*?" the schoolmaster asked wearily.

I never heard what they told him, because Joris looked at Helen and burst out laughing. Helen took a wisp of her hair away to look at me. She was laughing too.

"What's so funny?" asked someone.

"They don't understand!" I said. "They're having a joke on me! It's not fair! This could happen to anyone!"

Adam looked at me. It was a colorless, blank look, stony with suspicion. It shut me up at once. But it didn't shut Joris up. He kept bowing over and laughing. He went on doing it after the vehicle started and all the time the schoolmaster was driving us back towards the city. Joris was still red in the face and gurgling when the teacher called back over his shoulder, "Macready. Where do you and your gang want to be dropped?"

This meant Adam. Macready was his surname. He said, "I'll show you, sir," and went and stood behind the schoolmaster's shoulder. "This'll do, sir. By that lamp post."

The vehicle stopped. All the boys surged to their feet. Somebody lugged me along. Joris came too, still amused, like somebody who is coming along to watch the fun. That was one of the times I could have shaken Joris. He didn't see the trouble we were in at all. Helen clattered off the vehicle as well, at the end of the line. I hoped she could do something to help at least. The boys didn't know what to make of Helen at all. They tried to pretend she wasn't really there. They clustered in a group at the edge of a busy road, surrounding Joris and me, but leaving Helen standing out beyond, beside one of the trees that lined the street.

"Where to?" one of them asked Adam.

"Up here," Adam answered. "There's a lonely alley that will suit us perfectly."

I had been afraid there would be an alley. It was uncanny how the streets in this city were like mine. It was a broad street, with unusually broad pavements. In this world, there were trees lining the pavements and shops standing back behind the trees. In my world, this street was the worst part of the slums, with rubbish heaped on the broad pavements and tramps and ruffians camped out among the rubbish. You could get robbed in the alley. In this world, clean and orderly though it was, there was a tramp on the wide pavement too. He was asleep under the next tree along from Helen. I noticed him because my resisting feet were dragged round his dirty old boots as the boys pulled me towards the alley.

"I hope you meant that about tea, Adam," somebody said, as they pushed Joris and me up the steps that led to the alley.

"Sure," said Adam. "My parents are away for the weekend. They left loads of food. Just deal with these two yobboes first. I want them to know how it feels to have their clothes stolen."

By that I knew we were going to get robbed in

this alley too. I've told you what happens if people rob a Homeward Bounder. And, as if that weren't enough, I knew that the way to make Joris really fighting mad was to do something to his precious demon hunter's uniform.

X

Our many feet went clopper-popper inside the high red walls of the alley. It was like being marched off to an execution—only it was the firing-squad who were marching off to commit suicide. Without knowing they were.

"Look," I said, "I've told you you can have your trousers back. Take them."

"Ah, but I want your shirt too," said Adam.

"You can have it. I'll give it you," I said.

By now, we had got to a place where the alley curved, shutting us off from the view of anyone coming from either way. The boys stopped and dumped their clothes in a heap by the wall. Then they spread out so that there was a group round me and another round Joris.

"You are a coward, aren't you?" Adam said. He really disliked me. I felt the same about him.

"That's got nothing to do with it," I said. "You take anything of ours and you'll get killed. It's as simple as that. I don't care two hoots about you, but it seems a bit hard on the rest of them." I said that to try and make Joris understand about Rule Two. "It would be safer for you just to beat us up," I said. "We'd prefer that, wouldn't we, Joris?"

I couldn't tell what Joris thought. His mind worked on such different lines from mine. But I could see what the boys thought. They thought I was just trying to talk us out of it. They simply closed in.

Then I had to fight. It was the daftest situation. All the reasons were upside down. All the same, I went for Adam with a will, and tried to get his glasses off and stamp on them, while a whole crowd of others tried to get Adam's trousers off me.

Someone shouted, "Look out! He's got a knife!"

Everyone stampeded away backwards, with me in their midst.

That left Joris alone in a ring of us, standing in an expert-looking crouch. The knife Joris was holding looked very nasty. It was a thin glimmering prong, like a slice of glass. "This is a demon knife," Joris said. He was fighting mad all right. "I'll only have to touch you. Who comes first?" He followed up this invitation by advancing on the nearest boy.

"No! Stop it, Joris!" I shouted. "You can't! That's entering play!"

"Why should I keep *Their* rules?" said Joris. He glared round the ring of us as if we were all *Them*. Then he went crouching towards the nearest boy again, who flattened himself against the wall of the alley, terrified.

I remembered that it was only yesterday that

Joris had stood inside a ring of *Them*. I suppose this had taken him right back to it. I unwrapped what felt like sixteen boys' arms from my neck and arms. Joris raised the prong-like knife. I charged forward and tried to grab Joris.

Joris knew it was me. I could see from his face that he wasn't meaning to hurt me. But, the very instant I grabbed him, a loud, quavering voice cried out, "For shame! For shame! A man's hand against his brother!"

Joris jumped, and so did I. The knife stabbed down towards the terrified boy. And the next thing I knew, there was a sort of fizzle, and my left arm was pouring blood.

I clutched at my arm, trying to keep the cut closed, and leaned against the wall. I could see everyone staring at me in horror, Joris most of all. "It only takes a touch!" he said. "I've killed you!"

You say things you shouldn't say, when you've had a shock. I said, "Now you'll see what a mortal wound's like on a Homeward Bounder. I won't die, you fool. Rule One."

"I'm sorry," Joris said abjectly.

"Hope not to die! Hope not at all!" cried the quavering voice. It was the old tramp who had been asleep against the tree. Helen was with him. She had one side of her hair hooked up to stare at the blood running out of my arm. The sacred face looked unusually pale and upset. Beyond her, I could grayly see quite a few of the boys picking their clothes out of the heap and tiptoeing off. "Hope is an anchor, they say!" howled the tramp. "Indeed this is true. Hope you bear, bound to you like a millstone round the neck. I say cast it from you! Cast hope aside!"

I looked at the tramp, feeling decidedly gray and wavery, and slid down the wall until I was sitting on the ground. From down there, the old man looked truly disgusting. He had a whole bank of withered, wrinkled chins, loosely scattered with long strands of gray hair. Dirty white hair stuck up from under his filthy hat. His watery black eyes gleamed with a mad light, and his nose stuck out from below them, sharp and long and starved as the prow of the Flying Dutchman. I could tell he was a Homeward Bounder. That was why Helen had fetched him. But it was quite obvious that he was stark, raving mad too.

By this time, nearly all the boys had picked up their clothes and filtered away. I didn't blame them. What with the knife and the blood and the discovery that they were dealing with lunatics, the alley must have seemed to them the kind of place you forget about quickly. In fact, before the old tramp had said very much more, only Adam was left. Adam seemed to be trying to do something to my arm. It hurt. I pulled aside. "Leave me be."

"Hold still," Adam said. "You can stop the bleeding like this. Have you another handkerchief?"

I hadn't, of course. "Joris," I said. "Something to stop the bleeding."

Poor Joris. His face was cheesy-looking. He was carefully putting that knife of his into a sheath, but he stopped when I spoke to him. "Oh," he said. "As to that." And he felt inside his leather jerkin. In spite of everything, I started to laugh.

"If you cast hope aside," the old tramp lectured us, "then all evil is cast out with it. Love and beauty enter in and a new world dawns."

"What are you laughing at?" said Adam.

"Everything," I said. I leaned back and giggled. Helen knelt down beside me with both sides of her hair hooked back. By this time, Joris had done his conjuring trick and brought out a First Aid kit. Adam seemed to approve of it. He and Joris got to work with it on one side of me. Helen was on the other side. I suppose Helen thought they weren't attending to her, because the old tramp was still preaching away. But Adam was listening. I knew, because you can always tell, if someone is touching you. Their fingers go light and tense, not to interfere with what they're hearing.

"What happened?" Helen said. "*How* did it happen? I was looking straight at you, and Joris didn't even have his knife *near* you!"

"*Them,*" I said. "Another rule I hadn't noticed before. Joris ought to have got that boy against the wall. But he couldn't, because that would be entering play. It would have killed the boy. I suppose if I hadn't been near, he'd have had to stab himself." Then I burst out laughing again, for Adam's benefit.

They would make sure Adam didn't understand. I hoped he'd think we were all lunatics and creep away like the other boys.

The tramp broke off preaching and frowned at me. "Laugh not at the words of truth, my fellow exile," he said. "There is power in numbers."

"I wasn't laughing at you," I said.

"You are young in the ways of the worlds," stated the tramp, "old though you think yourself. Listen to me. Listen to the wisdom of Ahasuerus, who was among the first to have the Mark of Cain set on him."

I think that's how he said his name. It sounded like a sneeze. "Listen to who?" I said.

"Ahasuerus," said the old tramp. "That same whom they term the Wandering Jew."

At this, Adam finished with my arm and sat back on his heels, listening frankly.

"Never heard of you," I said. I wanted to shut the old fellow up. But all I seemed to do was set him off again. He was worse than Joris. He began again on all that stuff about hope and anchors—he knew *Them* all right, that was for sure—and all I could do was sit and stare at his dirty big toe poking out of the front of one of his cracked old boots, and wait for him to stop.

"I'm sorry I fetched him now," Helen muttered. "I thought he'd help."

"*They* gave me to hope," Ahasuerus said. "*They* hung me in hope as one in chains, and put a goal before me and set me on my way. But that goal always retreats from me, as mirage in the wilderness or star from star. I am weary now, and hope is a heavy burden. And *They* put a lie in my mouth, so that I may not tell the worlds about *Them*, but must say that I sinned against God. But this is a lie, and there is power in numbers. Before three of my own kind, I may speak the truth. For I was born with more sight than most, and I saw *Them*. I saw the gaming-board of *Them* and I saw the game *They* played with the nations. And I went out to preach and warn my people of *Their* coming ploy. And, for that reason, *They* took me, Ahasuerus, and hung chains upon me, and sent me forth with lies in my mouth, and I am called the Wandering Jew."

Having said all this, the tramp turned his watery black eyes particularly on Adam. "Have you heard and harkened to the words of Ahasuerus?" he asked him.

"Oh yes," Adam said, smiling politely. It was the smile you humor lunatics with. "Every word."

"Then my hope is lighter upon me," said the tramp. "These three will bear witness that I spoke the truth." He nodded round at Joris and Helen and me. "You three will soon be separated, one from another," he said to us. "*They* will not let wanderers be long in company together. Make good use of your time." Then, greatly to my surprise, because I could have sworn we'd be stuck with the old man for hours yet, he went shambling away down the alley.

Adam stared after him. "If he was telling the truth," he said, "he must be at least two thousand years old."

"He was mad as a hatter," I said hastily. "A nut case, bonkers, round the bend, flipped—"

"Yes, but you're not," said Adam.

"Yes, we are," I said. "Look at us. She hasn't got a face. He thinks he hunts demons. I steal trousers all the time. The fact is—"

Helen interrupted me. "Take no notice," she said to Adam. "Jamie can't help it. He's scared of the rules all the time."

I might have known Helen would let me down. "Scared?" I said. "And so I should be! So should you. You've just seen two of them working. Joris kills me, because he ought to have killed someone else. And I don't die, because I can't." I shouldn't have said any of this. But I was shaken to pieces by all that had happened. And my arm hurt.

"Exactly," Adam said. "I'd welcome an explanation."

Helen said, "We're all Homeward Bounders. So was the tramp."

"Shut up," I said. "He won't believe a word you say. They never do. They're not allowed to."

Adam stood up. "Try me," he suggested, in his coolest way. "If you can convince me, I'll let you keep those trousers."

I didn't answer. I wasn't going to make a fool of myself, even for a pair of trousers. Helen looked at

Joris for support. Joris was leaning against the wall, looking like I felt. He said to me, "You ought to have your arm in a sling. Will it heal?"

Before I could say that I'd had bigger holes in me than this, Adam said, "My house is near the end of this alley. We can find him a sling there."

Someone must have agreed to go to Adam's house. I didn't. I was feeling too gray. But I know we went there. I was feeling too gray to notice the house much, except that it was big and red, with trees in front. The first thing I properly remember is being in the front hall. There was a skeleton there. It was standing in the hall, looking at me.

"Meet Fred," Adam said.

Fred was the skeleton's name. It stood with its splay feet on a sort of plinth. On the plinth, there were gold letters: FREDERICK M. ALLINGTON.

"How beautiful!" said Helen. Fred was just her sort of thing.

"My father's a doctor," Adam explained. "I think I may be one too." We were in the kitchen by then, and Joris was tying up my arm in a kitchen towel. Joris had recovered enough now to keep saying how sorry he was. They made me sit in a chair and drink a mug of sweet tea. I remember looking round the kitchen unfavorably while I drank it. It was so clean and white. Nowhere ever has good kitchens like my world. Our kitchen at Home was brown and warm and cluttered, and you could make toast at the range, even in summer. This one might have been a hospital. There was no range. I couldn't see anywhere to make toast. Still, it was better than nothing. A lot of worlds don't have kitchens at all.

Then I came to myself to discover that Adam had by no means given up hope of finding out about us. You could hardly blame him. He had seen enough to make anyone curious. "I can tell you're all from different places," he said, fishing for information, "by the way you talk. Joris has an American accent—"

"I haven't," said Joris. "But I still have a Kathayack twang."

"Ah," said Adam. "Helen sounds foreign." He was right there. Helen spoke good English, but it wasn't her native language, and it showed. "I'd guess Helen was Pakistani," Adam fished on.

"The House of Uquar," Helen said scathingly, "is in Spithicar."

"And I'm dead common," I said, to stop Adam.

"I was going to say," Adam said, "that I can't place you at all, Jamie. Have a biscuit."

As soon as Helen realized I was trying to stop Adam, she began to tell him all about us, and about Homeward Bounders, and *Them*, and the ways of the worlds, while Joris waited eagerly in the wings, ready to talk about Konstam the moment Helen stopped. But Joris was disappointed. Adam didn't believe a word.

He laughed. "Pull the other one!" he said. "Haras-uquara! Demons! *Them!* You've all been watching too much telly."

"Well, you asked us to tell you," I said. I was really annoyed. It's funny the way your mind works. I ought to have been relieved that Adam didn't believe Helen, but I wasn't. All of a sudden, I was desperate for him to believe. I wanted an ordinary person to understand about Homeward Bounders, just this once. Before I knew it, I was casting about for something that might convince Adam.

There was Joris's slave mark. But Adam could say, like Helen, that anyone could get tattooed. There was that silly whistle thing I still had from Creema di Leema. But Adam had probably seen things like it in his world too. I fetched it out of my shirt pocket and showed it to him, and he had. He said you could buy them at the newsagent's down the street. But there was Helen's arm.

"Helen," I said. "Show him your gift."

Helen's nose and half one eye had been showing, but, when I said this, her hair fell down in front of them completely. "No," she said.

"Why not?" I said. She didn't answer. "Oh, come on!" I said. "It's the only thing that's going to convince him. Why not?"

One word came out of her hair. "Joris."

I looked at Joris, and Joris looked at me. Neither of us knew what this meant.

"If you mean her face is her gift," Adam said, "I've seen it. It looks like a face to me."

"No," I said. "It's something else. Helen, what

do you mean—Joris?"

The ready-to-bite look came through Helen's hair. "He'll think I'm a demon."

"But I won't! I can't. I can *see* you're not a demon!" Joris protested. "I promise I won't."

Helen's nose-tip reappeared. "All right. If you promise." She began rolling up her sleeve.

"Her arm is an arm too," Adam said.

"You wait," I said.

Helen did the elephant-trunk again. I think that was her favorite. She did it slowly too, so that Adam could see her normal brown skin turning into each gray wrinkle, further and further up her arm. Adam goggled. He was really impressed. But so was Joris, in a different way. Joris leaned back in his chair—he looked relaxed, but I could see he was tense all over—and his eyes went all narrow. He watched every movement of that trunk like a cat. I could see Helen's eyes too, bright and black, watching Joris between strands of hair.

When the elephant trunk curled up, showing there was no bone in it, Adam said, "I think I'm convinced." He sounded shaken. But I could hardly attend, because of the way Joris was looking. When I think, I suspect that that was the thing which really convinced Adam—Joris's reaction.

"There," Helen said defiantly, bending the pink nostrils of the trunk towards Joris. "Demons do that, don't they? Am I a demon, Joris?"

"I—don't know what you are," Joris said.

"Demons—demons do that all over. Do you?"

"Only one arm," said Helen. "Is it more spirit than body?"

"Yes," said Joris, watching the gray trunk narrowly.

"Well, I can't help it," said Helen.

"No, and I don't suppose demons can either," I said. "Come off it, Joris. You promised."

"I know," Joris said, in a quiet, firm, determined way. "But I think she is part-demon."

That was another time when I wanted to shake Joris. Helen sort of shut down. The elephant trunk grew into an arm again, from the top downwards. Then Helen pulled her sleeve down and sat there without a face. She wouldn't speak whatever I said.

I could see it made Adam quite uncomfortable. "Care to expand a bit?" he said to me. "On Homeward Bounders and the rules and so on?"

So I told him. Adam made more tea—which Helen wouldn't touch—while I did, and Joris waited for his turn. As soon as I stopped to drink, Joris started in. "Of course Konstam would tell this better than me," he said. "Konstam—"

I didn't mean to groan, but I did. A faint moan came from behind Helen's hair too. Now, you must have noticed that Adam was quick on the uptake. One side of his mouth gave a bit of a flicker, and he turned to Joris in a smooth way that I could tell was taking the Archangel. "Tell me all about Konstam," he said.

Naturally Joris did. After a solid half hour, if Adam hadn't known Konstam was ten foot tall and a Great God, he had only himself to blame. It came pouring out: Konstam, Konstam, Konstam. Mixed with it was the story of Adrac and *Them*, which I think was much more interesting. But the thing which really interested Adam was the fact that Joris had been a slave.

Adam got far more out of Joris about that than we had bothered to. Joris rolled up his sleeve and showed Adam the anchor mark, of course, but he also told Adam that it had been done at the slave mart when he was seven, because that was Kathayack State Law. Konstam and the two other Khans who had come to buy Joris there had not wanted him marked. But they were not allowed to take him out of the State without. Then he went on to tell Adam that, no, he had not been born a slave. His grandmother had sold him because the family was too poor to keep him.

"How much did your grandmother get for you?" Adam asked. He was commercial-minded, like me.

"Five thousand crowns," said Joris. "The Khans gave ten thousand."

Adam whistled. "Some profit! Are you still worth that much?"

"Twice as much," Joris said modestly. "I'd have been worth twice as much again when I was fully trained." He sighed. "Konstam—"

Adam nipped Konstam in the bud. He began pointing at things in the kitchen and asking Joris how many crowns they were worth. Before long, Adam's face was shining. "I make it a crown is worth slightly over a pound!" he said. "Are all slaves worth that much?"

"No," said Joris. "Only first-class boys. They get trained as runners or racing drivers. Girls go for a lot less when they're small, but they can go up in value later, if they turn out pretty."

"How much," said Adam, with bated breath, "for a pretty girl?"

"Well, it depends how well brought up they've been," said Joris, "and whether they've been taught music and dancing and massage—"

"Oh very well brought up," said Adam. "Knows everything."

"Then," said Joris, "a handsome virgin, with accomplishments, can go for up to sixty thousand crowns."

"Does," Adam asked eagerly, "color of hair and things like that make a difference to the price?"

"Red hair does," said Joris. "Because it's uncommon. Red hair can add as much as five hundred crowns to the price."

Adam wrapped his arms round himself and rolled about in his chair, in an agony of avarice. "Oh!" he said. "Oooh! Lead me to your world, Joris! The *money* I'd make! Of course, I'd have to get Vanessa there too, but I could manage that. Oh, if only we had slaves here! I'd sell Vanessa tonight!"

"Who's Vanessa?" I said.

"My sister," said Adam. "My sneering, bossy, know-all, redheaded sister. Next time she goes on at me, I shall sit and think how much I can sell her for. Ooh! Oh! Ah! Sixty thousand, five hundred pounds!"

This brought Helen's nose out into the open. "Greedy pig!" she said. "And I thought Jamie was commercial-minded!"

"Tell me about you," Adam said quickly to the nose, before it could go in again.

"I might," said Helen. And she put a mouse she had been nursing down on the table. The critter ran like clockwork towards the biscuits.

"I didn't know you kept mice," Adam said.

"I don't. It lives here," said Helen. "It's quite sweet, but I'd prefer it if you had rats." This was quite true, but what it meant was that Helen was still in a bad mood. It took me quite a while to coax her into telling Adam how she saw *Them* at *Their* game in the House of Uquar.

That story caused Adam to take his glasses off and twirl them about. He seemed to do that when he was thinking. I suspect that he thought a lot. His glasses were broken on both sides and mended with wire and sticking-plaster.

"Funny," he said, when Helen had finished. "You seem all to have seen *Them* differently. It's given me quite a few ideas. I'm not sure I like my ideas, either. But I know what kind of games *They* were playing. Like to come and see one?"

XI

Adam took us through the hall, past Frederick M. Allington the skeleton, and down some steps to a big basement room. Like all the rest of his house, it was beautifully polished and painted and well kept. Rich. Posh. Adam switched on a bright light over a large table in the middle of the room.

Even Helen recoiled. I jumped back. Joris had got right out of the door before Helen said, "It's only models. Come back, fool."

She was right. But, for a moment, I could have sworn it was one of *Their* game tables. There was a real-looking landscape built on the table. Adam said it was made out of paper and glue and paint mostly. He was proud of it. He had made most of it. There were hills, a wood, bushes, a lake, and some clusters of houses. Over this landscape were arranged the soldiers and machines and guns of a mud-brown war. All the little figures were beautifully painted, to look as real as possible. Adam had done those too.

"This is called a War Game," Adam said. "This

one's a modern war I'm in the middle of playing with my father." He went up to the table and looked over the arrangement of models. He picked up one of the rulers lying on the landscape and made some measurements. The intent way he did it made all three of us think of *Them*. "I think I've got him," he said. "When he comes back on Sunday, I'm going to crush him. It takes real skill, you know."

"Doesn't it depend on luck at all?" I said, nodding to the handful of dice lying near the rulers.

"*They* threw dice," Joris said. He was staring at that table just as he had stared at Helen's arm.

"You told me," said Adam. "You said *They* moved things on the table and sometimes threw dice after that. That was what made me sure it was War Gaming. You don't use the dice every move—that's why it takes skill—you use them to tell you the results of the battles, how many men get killed, and so on. We use dice for the weather too. We make it quite subtle. You can read the rules if you like." He picked up a fat booklet from the edge of the table and passed it to Joris.

Helen put her hair back to stare at the table of soldiers. That meant she was impressed. "But what do *They* use the machines for?"

"Calculating the odds on this or that move, I should think," Adam said. "Dad and I have often said we could do with a computer. Just think how much more you'd need one if you were playing with the whole world!" Adam's face took on a blissful, wistful look. "Fancy a War Game with the whole world for a table!"

"But where do *They* get the machines?" Helen persisted.

"How should I know?" said Adam. "Though what I'd do if I was *Them*, would be to let people invent them, on this world or that, and then kill the people off and take the machines myself."

"So would I," said Helen. "I think *They* do. But you may not be right. The game I saw *Them* playing in the House of Uquar wasn't like this."

"Yes, it was really," Adam assured her. "It was the kind we call Fantasy War Gaming. Any number of people can play that. Look. I can't show you it set out, because we play with just a referee and a map." He took Helen and me over to a shelf at one side of the room where there were piles of hand-drawn maps. They looked like mazes—or pictures of the travels of an earthworm. "These are underground maps," Adam explained, full of enthusiasm, "with masses of traps, pitfalls and monsters. Basically, the referee sets the players' men going through one of these places, and they see if they can fight their way out of it before something gets them. There's something horrendous every few yards."

"That's Helen's world!" I said.

"You made it sound like one of my outside Fantasy maps," Adam said, leafing through his heap. "Players can take over a fort in those. Oh, and a lot of emphasis is put on the endowments of the players' men—how strong they are, and how persistent, and whether they're fighting men or thieves or clerks, and what class of man or magic user they've got to. Is your world like that?"

"Yes," said Helen. "I am a cleric and a magic user." This was news to me, but, when I thought about it, what else could she have been?

Joris came up with the book of rules just then, looking puzzled. "This War isn't like ours with the demons, not really."

"No," said Adam. "From what you said, yours is a version of the game in Helen's world. That's why they threw dice so much. When a player's man meets a monster—or a demon—he's allowed a saving throw, to give him some kind of chance. We use these many-sided dice—"

"Some of *Their* dice had many sides," Joris said.

Helen said loudly, "I'm angry. How dare *They* play games!"

"Quite," said Adam. "What worries me is that this world—my world—has to be a game like the one on the table. And when *They* start playing *Their* next war, it's going to be a nuclear one. You know—radiation."

"Demon rays," Helen and Joris said together. I didn't say anything. I was remembering that Adam's world was ninth in a war series. My home was so like his, that it was probably tenth. *They* could be playing that kind of war there at the moment. Or worse—my Home could have been the world just before Adam's, the one with the demon rays. But I couldn't let myself think that. I couldn't!

Adam turned and opened boxes of different kinds of soldiers, red-coated, blue-coated, in armor, and in kilts. I don't think he was attending to them any more than I was. He had taken his glasses off to twiddle. "How does one get rid of *Them*?" he said.

But, just then there was a terrific clatter of feet, and someone with flaming red hair in a flaming rage came shooting down the steps into the basement. "Adam! *Adam!* I draw the *line* at pet mice on the kitchen table!" She was a grown-up lady, but she really was pretty, in spite of too much makeup and the rage she was in. She would have been worth every penny of sixty thousand crowns. "A tame mouse!" she shouted. "Eating biscuits on the table!"

"It wasn't tame," said Adam. "It was quite, quite wild. I hoped it would tear you to bits." And he said to us, "My sister. Vanessa." He had introduced Fred the skeleton in a much more friendly way.

"Oh you *would* have visitors!" said Vanessa. "You always do when I'm really mad with you!" She came towards us trying to pretend it was a joke. But it wasn't. I could see Adam really annoyed her.

Joris backed away from her. He was thoroughly embarrassed. He remembered the conversation about the price of handsome virgins as well as I did. Helen was ashamed about the mouse. Her hair came down like a curtain. Which left me standing out in front.

Vanessa wasn't very tall. Even with the high-heeled shoes ladies wore in Adam's world, she wasn't much taller than me or Adam. That made me feel I knew her quite well, somehow. Her face, the same level as mine, lost its annoyance and its false smile as soon as she looked at me. She looked at my arm in the kitchen towel, and she looked back at my face. "What's been happening to you? You look really ill!"

"It's a long story," I said. "I had a bit of an accident."

"It was me—" began Joris.

"Not to worry," Adam cut in quickly. "Joris and me gave him First Aid. He's Jamie, by the way. This is Helen, the one without a face."

It was no good. Vanessa was used to Adam. She just stuck to her point. "Let me look at it at once," she said to me. "Adam doesn't know the first thing—"

"I do," Joris said timidly, and Adam said, "I *do*!" but Vanessa took not the blindest bit of notice of either. She simply dragged me off to a place where there were a great many strong-smelling medicines and bandages and things. While she stripped off the kitchen towel, she told me she was nineteen and had just started training to be a doctor, so I could have every confidence. Then she saw the cut. It gave her rather a shock—demon knives are pretty vicious things—and she wanted to rush me off to the hospital at once to have it stitched.

I refused to go. I knew it would mean no end of trouble in a well-organized world like this one. I thought they would probably end up putting me in a madhouse. So I talked and talked at Vanessa to persuade her to forget about the hospital. I haven't the faintest memory of what I said. It's a funny thing—if people get sympathetic and start worrying about you, you always feel twice as ill. I felt really gray. I remember talking, and Vanessa answering in a humoring sort of way, but I've no idea what I said. But it turns out I told her all about Adam and the game and the alley, and half my life as a Homeward Bounder as well. Helen swore I did, so I suppose I must have done. I must have thought Vanessa wouldn't believe a word.

Anyway, she put a dressing on my arm and made it much more comfortable. Then she made me go and lie down in their front room. I thought of it as their parlor—we'd have called it a parlor at Home. It had smart velvet chairs and a piano and wax fruit and photographs of relatives, just as ours did. But I think they called it a living room. That was daft, because the room was much posher than our parlor. Even the relatives in the photographs were all much posher than ours—imposing old fellows in whiskers and ladies in a lot of hat. There was one photograph of a lady in a hat just over the smart sofa I was lying on, and I kept staring at it. The lady didn't look at all like Vanessa—when do relatives in photos ever look like anyone alive?—but I kept thinking I'd seen her before. I dozed off, and woke up, and looked at the photographed lady several times, and each time she looked more familiar.

The rest of them thought I was asleep all the time. They kept creeping in, pretending they were having a look at me, in order to have private talks.

I woke up to hear Adam whispering. "That knife just leaped at him. I've never seen anything like it! Joris thought he'd killed him. He is OK, isn't he?"

"Yes, but it's a nasty cut," Vanessa whispered back. "I wish he'd go to the hospital. Adam, don't slide off. Have they told you—? If all this about *Them* is true, oughtn't we to do something?"

"I know we ought!" Adam whispered. "It's serious. I'm not going to sit about waiting to be someone's toy soldier."

"Or some*thing*'s," said Vanessa.

"Too right!" said Adam.

A bit later on, I opened my eyes to look at the lady in the photograph and heard Joris talking: "... all my fault," he was saying, "because it was a silly joke between me and Helen. Only Helen won't talk to me now, so can I talk to you?"

"Yes, if you want," Vanessa said. "But don't wake Jamie up."

"Helen says Jamie kept getting her into messes," said Joris. "She said he showed off. But I don't think that was fair, because Jamie *does* know. It was my fault. I took too long stealing a coat, and then I lost my head in the alley. I hate myself. And there's another thing."

"What is that?" said Vanessa.

Joris said, "I think slavery is wrong."

"Well," said Vanessa, "you should know."

"No, but I don't," said Joris. "Not from my own experience. Konstam never treats me like a slave. Konstam—"

Once he was on Konstam again, I went straight back to sleep. I was amused. I could see Joris was trying to warn Vanessa about Adam's plans for her. I wondered what made him so sure that being a slave would be a bad thing for Vanessa, if it wasn't for him.

The next time I woke up and looked at the familiar lady in the photograph, it was because someone was crying. I moved round very gently and sort of stretched my eyes sideways to see who it was. I thought it was Joris again, to tell the truth. But it was Helen! I was shocked. I hadn't thought Helen *could* cry. But there she was, sitting on the sofa across from mine, with her hands to her face, howling her eyes out. Vanessa was sitting on the floor beside the sofa with both arms round Helen. I thought, poor Vanessa! She's having quite a time among all of us!

"It's *not* a gift!" Helen howled. "It's a d-d-deformity! It's not even properly a body! Joris said it wasn't."

"Yes, but Joris was thinking of his own world," Vanessa said. "I'm sure you can't judge one world by another. Helen, you'd be much better thinking of it as a gift you haven't found the use of yet. Haven't you ever been given a present like that? You can't think what to do with this gadget you've been given, but you know it'll come in handy for something."

Helen managed to laugh and cry at once. "That's clever! I'll call my arm my gadget in future. What made you think of it?"

"Because I feel a bit like that myself," Vanessa said. "I'm going to be a doctor, because that's what everyone is in my family, but there are all sorts of bits of me that I won't be using for that. And I keep thinking they must come in handy sometime."

"I hope they do," Helen said, sniffing.

Vanessa said, "Better now?"

"Yes," said Helen. She went all fierce. "I shall use my gadget to exterminate *Them*, because of what *They* did to Jamie!"

A bit later on, Adam came and woke me up. "Vanessa says can you eat some supper when she's cooked it?"

"Sure," I said. "I could even eat that wild mouse. Adam, who's that lady with the hat in that photo up there?"

Adam pushed his glasses up his nose to see. "Oh, her. That's my great-grandmother they've bored me with ever since I can remember. She was one of the first ever women doctors, or something. There's more pictures of her in that album over there, if you want to look."

"Depends how soon supper is," I said.

"Ten minutes," Adam said. He fetched me the album. "I warn you," he said, "they're all either her and a potted fern, or her cutting up a corpse. She only looks human in the first one. She was about fifteen in that one. They say she probably looked quite like Vanessa. Red hair photographed as black in those days."

He went away, and I opened the album. I knew why the lady looked familiar at once. The apparently black-haired girl staring solemnly out of the first photograph was indeed like Vanessa, only not so pretty. Vanessa was older, of course. This girl was at the prim and fussy stage. You could see she'd fussed for hours about her clothes to be photographed in. But, even so, even more than Vanessa, that girl reminded me of my sister, Elsie—she reminded me so much of Elsie that I took a look at her feet, expecting to see Rob's cast-off boots on them. But of course she was wearing elegant little pointed shoes, of a kind my parents could never have afforded.

I didn't bother to look at the rest of the album. When Helen came to say supper was ready, she said, "Whatever's the matter, Jamie?"

I swallowed what felt like half my throat. "You behaved awfully well," I said, "that time in the pantomime horse, when you thought you'd seen your mother. I wouldn't have been nearly so sensible."

"I knew you were right," said Helen. "Why?"

I showed her the photograph. "That could almost be my sister, Elsie," I said. "This world's so like mine that I think mine may even be next one on."

"Then why didn't you *say* so?" said Helen. "You

shouldn't have let us make you stay here! I'll go and tell Joris, and we'll move on tomorrow."

That cheered me up wonderfully. Supper cheered me up more, even though Vanessa was a really rotten cook. It turned out that Helen and Joris had helped Vanessa cook—in which case I shudder to think what Vanessa's food was like when she cooked it on her own. While we ate it, Joris talked about Konstam. He talked nonstop. He had two new listeners in Vanessa and Adam, and he made the best of them.

"Does he ever stop?" Adam muttered to me.

"He hasn't yet," I said. "But he's only been on the Bounds two days."

"Adam, it's rude to whisper," said Vanessa.

"Who's a pink-haired trout then?" said Adam.

"You disgusting blind toad!" retorted Vanessa.

It amazed me how rude they were to one another. They didn't insult one another for fun, either. They both really meant it. But, when they stopped snarling insults, they seemed perfectly good friends. The sudden changes made me nervous. The third time they went at one another, they actually stopped Joris talking. There was total silence when they stopped.

"Sorry about that," said Adam. He wasn't sorry at all. "Jamie, we want to do something about *Them*. We think we've discovered some weak points in *Their* rules."

They had been discussing it while I was asleep.

Adam had made a list of every single fact Helen or Joris knew about *Them*, and they had all remembered the things I had said. Then Adam had thought about it, hard.

"First," he said, "*They* make the rules, and then the rules seem to work automatically, by themselves—as in a certain incident in a certain alley. Second, you lot are what *They* call random factors. Now that ought to mean something quite unpredictable, which crops up in spite of the rules. But I think *They* use it to mean more than that. What's the main thing you three have in common?"

"We've seen *Them* playing," I said.

"Right," said Adam. "And once you did, you were disconnected from the game—neutralized as Homeward Bounders. And all sorts of new rules came into operation to make sure you stayed that way. Why?"

"Because otherwise we'd tell ordinary people like you," I said, "and you'd want to do something about *Them*."

"Yes, that's what *They* want you to think," said Adam. "But you're forgetting part of Helen's story. Helen's teacher couldn't see *Them*."

I felt my mouth come open. I shut it quick. It was full at the time. What my mother would have said! "Then what are *They* playing at? You mean most people can't see *Them* at all?"

Adam's face gleamed with enthusiasm. "That's right! I know how it works! It's brilliant! I wish it was possible in ordinary War Gaming! It adds an extra game on the side, and turns *Their* game into a huge exciting gamble. What happens is that you prove that you can see *Them* and you become a Homeward Bounder in an enormous game of chance, like *Ludo* or *Snakes and Ladders* or something, going on round the edge of the War Game. Think. There are hundreds, or maybe millions of people wandering about who know what's going on. If these people come together with the right people at the right time, they can ruin everything for *Them*. Actually, the odds are on *Their* side. Think how many odds there must be against you three first coming together, then coming here, finding me, convincing me, and me happening to know about War Gaming — out of millions of worlds and millions of people who don't! But it can happen. It just has. And now it has, we can win the game and bring *Them* down."

"Yes," I said. "But you forget *They* know. *They* know everything."

"But we still think we can do something," Vanessa said. "I'm sure we can. This is my idea. There are only allowed to be a certain number of Homeward Bounders, aren't there? By the time Joris was — er — discarded, there was only room for one more after him. Maybe *They*'ve sent someone else off since. Anyway, the numbers are nearly full. So I think we ought to increase that number — overload the circuit, and see what happens."

I didn't see it. I mean, I understood all right, but Vanessa didn't know *Them*. *They*'d just make the numbers right somehow—probably kill off old Ahasuerus or the Flying Dutchman, or one of us. I didn't say it, though. I said, "What do you aim to do?"

"I think," said Vanessa, "that Adam and I have become random factors because we believe you. I think we should leave notes explaining all about *Them* to our parents, to make it thoroughly difficult for *Them*, and come with the three of you when you move on tomorrow."

"I think that's what Ahasuerus meant," said Helen.

"So when do the Bounds call next?" Adam asked.

"We don't need to wait for the call," Joris pointed out.

Then they all looked at me to see what I thought. I still couldn't say. It wasn't only that I was twice as scared of *Them* than even Joris was. It wasn't only that I didn't like to say it was no use. What had suddenly got me was that I didn't know when the Bounds were going to call next in this world. I hadn't a clue. We seemed to have messed things up by going through Boundaries on our own. And that put me in a taking. Suppose the Bounds called suddenly— tonight—I would have to go to the nearest Boundary. And I knew the nearest Boundary couldn't be those vegetable patches. That was too far away. But those vegetable patches were the only Boundary where I could be reasonably sure of getting to my own Home. I didn't know what to do.

I must have looked gray again. Vanessa said, "We'll put you to bed, Jamie, and decide properly tomorrow morning. Adam's supposed to have school on Saturday mornings, but I expect a mysterious illness to strike him any moment. We shall have all tomorrow and most of Sunday to take action in. You sleep on it."

I did sleep on it. I slept in a vast bed belonging to Adam's parents, under a thing I'd have called an eiderdown. Adam called it a duvet. Very posh. It must have taken a whole farmyard full of hens to stuff that thing. I sweltered. So did Joris. He was in the other side of the vast bed in the morning, and the hot eiderdown was piled up between us, and I hadn't even known he was there.

I lay for a while when I woke up, thinking it was lucky the Bounds hadn't called in the night. I'd been too fast asleep to hear them.

"How are you?" said Joris, when he saw I was awake.

I felt good. My arm hardly hurt at all. "All right," I said. "Joris, what do *you* think of Vanessa's idea for getting rid of *Them*? Do you think it could be that simple?"

Joris considered. I could see in his face the horror of *Them*. He'd had *Them* a good bit more recently than me, after all. "No," he said. "It can't be right. Helen says your world is next one on. I think we should go there."

"Thanks!" I said. I was really relieved. "Let's sneak off straight after breakfast then."

But we never got a chance. Joris and I were just coming downstairs, wondering what people ate for breakfast in this world, when the doorbell rang. We didn't know it was the doorbell. It made a gentle chime—*ping-pong*. We only realized what the noise was when Adam drifted across the hall, looking like someone from Creema di Leema in yellow pajamas with purple spots, and went out of sight round the corner to open the front door. . . .

We heard Adam make a sort of *glunk*-noise. Someone outside said, "Forgive me. I have a hot reading for this house." And then a man dressed just like Joris leaped energetically into the middle of the hall.

Joris let out a huge shout of *"Konstam!"* and came rushing downstairs so fast that I had to rush too in order not to be knocked over.

Yes, it was Konstam Khan. Ten-foot Konstam himself. I didn't believe it at first, any more than you do. But he was really there, standing just in front of Fred the skeleton, with his white boots planted wide apart on the hall carpet, looking anxiously at Joris. But when he saw Joris rushing at him in one piece, he smiled, showing amazingly white teeth, and his face sort of glowed. He put the little square instrument he had been carrying away in the front of his white leather jerkin—which had the same black sign on it as Joris's—and began stripping off his white leather gauntlets. He hung the gloves in his belt, beside the curved sword and the holstered gun which were already there.

"Joris, I'm sorry to have been so long coming to fetch you," Konstam said.

By this time, Vanessa was in the doorway of the kitchen in a trailing blue dressing-gown, and Helen was on the stairs behind me. We all stared at Konstam.

Because the amazing thing about Konstam Khan was that he really was all the things that Joris said he was. You only had to look at him to see he was. You could tell he was brave and strong and heroic from the way he held his head and the way he moved—he moved so lightly that it was plain he had muscles most people don't even get born with. He had godlike good looks too. His skin was very brown, browner than Helen's. And one of the things which made Konstam so handsome was the faint glow of pink through the brown of his cheeks. I always liked that in Helen, but she only had that when she was in a good mood. Konstam glowed with health all the time. His blue-black hair waved crisply from his face. His black eyes flashed with health and keenness. He was considerate, and he was nice. You could tell that from the way he looked at Joris. He had that nice, straight way of looking that Joris had.

In fact, he was as godlike as Joris had said—except for one thing. He was nothing like ten feet tall. He was about an inch shorter than Joris was.

I saw Joris notice Konstam's height as he rushed at Konstam. It obviously surprised him. Behind Joris's back, Adam put one hand as high as he could in the air, and then lowered it expressively to dwarf-height. I had to turn away and snore. Vanessa hid her face in the doorjamb.

"But Konstam, how did you do it? How did you get here? How did you find me?" Joris clamored.

"I knew you'd no means of getting back on your own," Konstam said. "The trouble was, Adrac took you through so many worlds that you went right off the range of the portable tracker. I had to fly home and trace you from Khan Valley. That's what took the time. But you must have known I'd come and fetch you." Konstam obviously didn't feel it was worth explaining how he had come skipping from world to world. I suppose he'd done it like we did with Joris.

"I—" Joris began, beaming with delight. Then he went all anxious and looked at me. "I—I can go Home, can't I? Does being a Homeward Bounder stop you?"

"Of course you can go," I said. "Didn't you listen to *Them*? If you can get Home, you can reenter play." I envied Joris. Oh, I envied him. Envy turned my stomach round, the moment I saw Konstam. No one had been able to come and fetch me.

Up to then, Konstam had obviously been thinking of nothing but Joris. You could see he had been worried sick about him. Now he looked round and made a little bow to us all, with a lower bow to Vanessa. He thought she was probably the lady of the house. Joris looked embarrassed again. I could tell he was thinking of the sixty thousand crowns.

"I'm afraid I rather barged in," Konstam said. "Do forgive me."

"We're very glad to see you," Vanessa said politely. "We've heard *such* a lot about you. Would you care for some breakfast now you're here?"

"Could I have some breakfast, Konstam, before we go?" Joris asked humbly.

"Of course," Konstam said. And he said to Vanessa, "I'd love a cup of tea, if your world has such a thing."

We were all rather sad, I think. We knew Konstam meant to take Joris Home straight after breakfast. But, as it turned out, he didn't. That was because, over breakfast, Joris told Konstam about *Them*.

XII

At first the story came tumbling out of Joris, all mixed up and helter-skelter, in the same way Joris had talked about Konstam. But Konstam said, "For goodness sake, Joris. Take a deep breath and then tell it logically." And Joris did.

I'd noticed before that when Joris had talked about demon hunting, or Boundaries, or anything to do with his trade, he always told it much more clearly. I think that was Konstam's doing. But Konstam only corrected Joris in the way anyone older than Joris would have done. That was another thing that turned out to be true—Konstam really didn't treat Joris like a slave. He seemed to like Joris a lot. It was quite clear, from the first minute when Joris came rushing downstairs, that Konstam had not come after Joris just because he was valuable property gone missing. No. The slave-stuff was all in Joris's head. Or, if you like, in a small anchor-shaped mark on his arm.

"What?" Konstam said, when Joris got to *Them.*

Joris repeated it as he had said it to us. "It must

have been in the spirit world. And I knew I was done for. There were so many of *Them*, and I could see *They* were all demons."

Konstam shook his crisp black head. "You were never in the spirit world. The tracker would have registered it. What *is* this? A place of demons — greater than *Adrac*! — gaming with worlds!"

"I swear it's true," said Joris. "Helen and Jamie have seen it too."

Konstam turned to me, looking almost feverish, his eyes glittered so. I saw the main thing about Konstam then. He was obsessed with demon hunting. It was his passion. The thought of a whole new set of demons he hadn't known about nearly drove him mad. He was as bad as Adam over the sixty thousand crowns.

Adam, by the way, spent the entire breakfast looking from Konstam to Vanessa and practically licking his lips.

So I told Konstam that it was indeed true about *Them*. Helen bore me out, without so much as letting the tip of her nose out through her hair. She was afraid Konstam was going to start hunting her too. I decided to have a word with Konstam about that. By then it was clear that Konstam was not going home yet. He had prodded and questioned at me so feverishly about how I came to see *Them*, that I ended up admitting that this city was very like the one which was my Home. Then it was no trouble at all to get me to admit that I could probably find the place where *They* were here too.

He leaped up and whirled to the middle of the kitchen. He was a great leaper, was Konstam. He never just walked if he could leap. "Come on then. Let's go and take a look at *Them*, Jamie!"

"Wait a minute!" Vanessa said, jumping up too. "Let me get dressed. I want to come."

"And me," said Adam.

"I beg your pardon," Konstam said to Vanessa, laughing a little. "I thought you were already dressed. I've been admiring your gown."

"I'm going to wear trousers," Vanessa said, and raced off, rather pink.

Adam paused in the doorway, to ask Konstam bluntly, "Are you very rich?"

"Fairly," Konstam said, looking puzzled.

"Good!" said Adam, and raced off too.

In the end, we all went to find *Them*. I don't think Joris and Helen wanted to in the least, but Joris was back to being Konstam's slave and he had to go, and Helen was afraid the Bounds might call while she was alone. I was glad of their company. I didn't want to see *Them* either. But Konstam was like that. He could make you do things wild horses couldn't drag you to.

Vanessa said she would drive us. There was a little old vehicle in a shed beside the house. Vanessa called it her car. In my world, *car* is a poetic word for a chariot. I stared at the thing. There was nothing poetic about it that I could see—my father's precious tricycle was more poetic. Joris was staring at it too. I remembered that he had said Konstam drove an expensive fast car, and I had thought he had meant something golden, drawn by a team of Thoroughbred horses. So I asked him whether this car was anything like Konstam's. Not really, Joris said, though he thought they both worked the same way.

"Is Konstam's more poetic, would you say?" I said. And Joris said, with great feeling, that it was, much more.

How six of us got in that unpoetic car, I shall never know. I was crammed in, in front, on top of Adam, as guide. My arm was really hurting again, from the crush, even before we were moving.

It took ages to find the place. For one thing, that city was quite a bit different from mine, in the place where it mattered, down by the canal arches. For another, it was annoyingly over-organized. I hate places with so many rules. You could only go one way along half the roads. We kept having to turn right, away from the canal, whenever I wanted to turn towards it. Vanessa drove round and round, and I began to think that *Their* place didn't exist here in her world. I ought to have felt glad, but I didn't, because Konstam got so dreadfully polite. Konstam was one of those who gets polite instead of angry. He frightened me to death.

We found it in the end. It was just round the corner from the new concrete station where we got off the train. I craned to look up at it as we buzzed past, and it was uncannily like the Old Fort in my Home. It was triangular, and made of pinkish stone with fort-like castellations, and it had the same shut, massive door. But there were no harpoons in front. Vanessa stopped the car when I shouted, just past the side street that ran beside *Their* park or garden. We all got out and went down the side street. That took me right back. It was so much the same that I almost expected to see a box of groceries standing beside the pink stone wall. I was scared.

They had to help me over the wall. My arm wouldn't work well enough for me to climb by myself. But that was no trouble to someone as strong as Konstam. He could have thrown me over it.

Over the wall, the silence hit us. There was a triangular park there too, with the same sort of dip in the middle, but there were not so many trees. The place was a mass of bushes, particularly up near the wall. And, as soon as we were standing among the bushes, all the instruments Konstam and Joris had began to register wildly. Their demon-indicators went right up to the ends of their scales and stayed there. The queer silence was broken by a faint *tut-tutting* from Joris's Boundary-finder too, and when he took it out, the needle was jumping faintly. But when he turned it over, the Boundary needle on the other side was swirling round almost too fast to see.

"This is very odd," Konstam whispered. "I've never met anything like this!" He could hardly wait to clap eyes on *Them*. He went so fast among the bushes that the rest of us had a hard time keeping up. At least, we could have kept up if we had gone further down the dip where there was open grass and run, but Konstam wouldn't hear of that. He turned and looked at Adam, when Adam tried to, and Adam didn't try again.

That way, we missed seeing all but a glimpse of the small white statue down in the dip. I was glad. By the time we were level with it, we were all distracted anyway because the demon hunters' instruments were making such a noise, whining and clicking and tut-tutting. Konstam stopped and switched them all off. Then he crept on, really cautiously. I am ready to swear that none of *Them* saw us.

There *They* were, almost as I saw *Them* at Home, across the gravel and dimly behind the reflections in the glass. Two of *Them* in gray cloaks. One of *Them* was delighted by what the machines seemed to tell him. He rubbed his hard-to-see hands. The other one seemed annoyed. From the look of *Them*, and from what Adam and Vanessa had been saying about their world, I thought *They* were playing small skirmishes as moves to lead up to a big war. But I don't know for sure, because I couldn't see the table through that window, and there was no point asking Adam. Adam couldn't see *Them* at all.

"I can't see *anything*! There's only reflections in the glass!" he kept whispering, over and over again, until Konstam turned round and frowned. That shut Adam up.

I have seen cats watch mouseholes the way Konstam watched *Them*. He was alert and quite still, and tense and greedy and murderous. Until he had suddenly seen enough and signaled all of us to get back. When we were all by the wall again, he said, "Right. Council of war. May we return to your house, Vanessa?"

"Of course. But it's my parents' house really," Vanessa said. She had gone white. Most people look ghastly like that, but Vanessa actually looked prettier. "We've got to stop *Them*!" she whispered. "I could feel how awful *They* were, even through the window."

"Could you? In that case you would make a good demon hunter," Konstam whispered.

Vanessa was very surprised. "Can women be demon hunters?"

"Gracious, yes!" Konstam said, as we all began to struggle over the wall. "Most of the best demon hunters are girls. Joris's friend Elsa is almost as good as Joris is. Isn't that so, Joris?"

Joris was on top of the wall, trying to haul me up. He was being all pale and businesslike. I suppose, now Konstam was here, *They* were like just another job to him. But he went a bit pink as he answered. "Elsa's pretty good," he said. I did wish there were no people called Elsa. The name made me sick for Home.

I don't know how Helen felt. She stayed inside her hair whenever Konstam was anywhere near her.

But Adam was really peevish. As soon as we had scrambled down into the sudden noise of the side street, he started going on about not being able to see *Them*. "It's not fair!" he said. "I thought it was going to be Vanessa who couldn't, not *me*. I suppose it proves I was right that most people can't see *Them*, but I thought it was going to be Vanessa who proved it. It's not fair!"

When we were all crammed into that car and Vanessa was driving us back, Konstam made me tell him, several times over, exactly what I had seen when I went into the Old Fort in my world. When we got to the house, he gathered us all round the kitchen table and did his flashing smile at us.

"Now," he said. "Council of war. Joris and I are going to have to go in after *Them*. We wouldn't be demon hunters if we didn't. *They* are clearly a new kind of extremely powerful demon. *They* have a massive corporeal part, which is usually quite unheard-of in demons that strong, and that's going to mean thinking up a new approach. I'd welcome any suggestions the rest of you can give us. For a start, there's the question of where *They* are. *They*'re not in the spirit world. I'm not even sure *They* could get into the spirit world in *Their* present corporeal state. On the other hand, *They*'re not in this world either."

"Then where the blazes are *They*?" I said.

"In the Real Place," said the voice behind Helen's hair. "Remember? I told you about the place of glass and reflections, Jamie. I'd always thought the Real Place was a person's own world. I thought that each world was the Real Place for the people living in it. But I looked at *Them* in that building and I suddenly knew it wasn't. *They* were in the Real Place there. I think *They*'ve stolen it from people."

"Thank you," Konstam said respectfully. But Helen wouldn't speak to him. "I'm sure Helen's right. And it looks as if this Real Place of *Theirs* seems different in different worlds. You all saw different versions. But this Place suits us quite well. If, as Jamie says, it's divided into triangular compartments in this cluster of worlds, we can go in and clean *Them* out of this triangle, and perhaps the next few, without taking on the whole lot. Then, when we've done that, and worked out the right way of dealing with *Them*, we can go home and muster all the demon hunters—Khans, Altunians, Smiths, Obotes, everyone—and start a major campaign."

That was another thing about Konstam. The idea of failing never occurred to him. He had looked at *Them*. He had seen *Them* as a problem and he set about solving it. His face glowed. I did try to suggest that *They* were a little more than just a problem, but I got swept away in the general enthusiasm. Konstam was like that. His confidence was catching.

Before long, we had all agreed to take part in the assault on *Them*. I even found that I had. Konstam was very pleased. That meant we would be three to each of *Them*. That way, Konstam thought we might be able to kill the bodily part and the spirit part both at once, and prevent *Them* taking a dive to the spirit world, where, even Konstam admitted, we would have our work cut out to do anything with *Them*. The stumbling block was that *They* were in the Real Place and not likely to come out. We would have to go in. No one was sure quite how to do that—we had to suppose, you see, that *They* would know we were trying to get in and be ready to stop us. But Konstam was sure we could solve that. Meanwhile, he set about getting us all properly equipped. He drew up a list.

"This is going to take a good bit of money," Joris said, looking it over.

Konstam smiled merrily and felt inside his leather jerkin. He seemed to have more things in there even than Joris. "I've thought of that," he said, and brought out a big coiled fistful of shining yellow wire. "I came prepared."

"Demon wire?" said Joris, as if this was an awful waste.

"Yes, I know," said Konstam. "But gold *is* gold. I thought I might have to buy you back from someone. Do you have such things as pawnbrokers in this world?" he asked Vanessa.

"I—think so," said Vanessa. "But any jeweler will give you a good price for gold at the moment."

You should have seen Adam's face when he realized Konstam was holding a fistful of solid gold! Now he knew Konstam was rich. I began to get quite worried about Vanessa. Konstam was pretty struck with her anyway. I had been noticing that from the start. And he obviously didn't see anything wrong with owning slaves or he wouldn't have bought Joris.

It was me who went out with Konstam to sell the gold. I had sold gold on several other worlds. Konstam was quite ready to take my advice. He put on an old raincoat belonging to Adam's father to disguise his demon hunter's uniform. Unlike Joris, he didn't seem to value it at all. But in spite of that we ran into trouble.

"Where did you get this, sir?" the jeweler asked when Konstam showed him the wire.

"I use it in my work," Konstam explained.

Oh, the rules and strictness of that blessed world! If the gold had been in any other shape but wire, it seems there would have been no trouble. But because it was wire, the dealer was sure it couldn't belong to Konstam. And Konstam, who had twice the sense of Joris, knew better than to explain about demons. In the end, the jeweler made Konstam sign a paper to say the wire was his, and we had to leave our names and Adam's address. Fuss, fuss! But he gave us quite a bit of money for it.

We bought some of the things we needed on the way back, but not all. I spent the rest of the day being sent out for other things. Back in the house, it was like a workshop. You couldn't buy demon equipment in that world at all. They had demons, Adam said, but they didn't believe in them, so they weren't a problem. This meant that Konstam and Joris had to make most of the things on the list themselves, out of metal and leather and wood and plastic, and any other material I could buy. Don't ask me what the things they made were. I didn't know what a trisp, or a nallete, or a conceptor was, any more than you do, and I still don't. I was just the errand boy.

Konstam and Joris did most of the making, because they knew what they were supposed to be doing, but they soon had Adam hard at it too, because he was so good at making things. Vanessa did the unskilled work. Helen came with me at first. When the various things were done, they hung them on Fred the skeleton. Konstam said Fred was a very good place to hang them, being human bones.

I didn't mind doing the shopping at all. It took my mind off Home and off *Them*. But I was nervous about what was going on while I was away. I was darn sure that, sooner or later, Joris would blurt out to Konstam about Helen's arm and that Konstam would decide Helen needed hunting too. And I was just as sure that, while my back was turned, Adam would offer to sell Vanessa to Konstam for sixty thousand, five hundred crowns. And I was quite right.

I came into the kitchen with a bundle of assorted knives and a paper bag of aluminium blocks. It must have been exactly one second after Adam made his offer. Joris and Vanessa were off ransacking Dr.

Macready's surgery again—Konstam was using everything there that was any use: he said he'd pay for anything he took—and that had left Adam alone with Konstam. The moment I came into the kitchen was the moment Konstam seized Adam. He slung Adam on the table and started to try and beat the pants off him. Konstam did it in such a cool and professional way that I couldn't help wondering how often he had done it before.

I backed delicately out of the kitchen, with the pounding ringing in my ears, and ran into Joris in the hall. "Er—does Konstam do this often?" I said.

Joris shook his head. He was horribly ashamed. "I think Adam was asking seventy thousand," he said.

A second later, Adam shot away upstairs, carrying the two halves of his glasses. Konstam shot to the door after him, really angry. He was going to shout something after Adam, when he saw Joris and me. "Oh good," he said. "You got some knives."

So we never did know how much Adam had tried to sell Vanessa for. Konstam was not saying—and not buying either, evidently. Adam stayed upstairs sulking until Joris and I went up and mended his glasses for him. We did it with a scrap of gold demon wire Joris happened to have, to console Adam a little. But Adam was not saying what he'd said to Konstam either. All he said was, "Joris, you have my hearty sympathy, belonging to that brute Konstam." Which offended Joris. Joris was very touchy all day anyway. Vanessa said she thought Joris was dreading going after *Them*. He probably was. He knew what *They* were like even better than I did.

When I came downstairs again, the other disaster had struck. Helen came racing into the hall, and Konstam came leaping after her.

"No—wait!" Konstam was saying.

"Don't you dare come near me!" Helen shouted. And she took hold of me and swung me round so that I was between her and Konstam. "Jamie, Joris *told* him!"

Well, I knew he would. "Leave her alone," I said to Konstam. "She's not even half a demon. If you touch her, I'll set *Them* on you!"

He stood looking at me as if he was exasperated. "I wasn't trying to hurt her," he said. "I just wanted to look at her arm."

That sounded pretty sinister to me. I suppose it was because we were in a doctor's house. "With a view to amputation?" I said. "You try!"

Konstam folded his arms and took a glance at the ceiling, and then at Fred hung with queer objects. He tapped with his white boot. "Jamie," he said patiently, "you've been in many more worlds than I have. Haven't you learned to judge people better than this?"

"I've learned enough to know you put demon hunting in front of anything else," I said.

"Yes," he said. "I do. That's why—Listen, I think

Helen is our means to get in at *Them*. You've seen her arm. Read this and see if you think so." He fetched a little floppy book out of his jerkin and passed it to me. "Page thirty-four."

The book was called *Mim's List 1692*. 1692 was this year's date in Konstam's world. When Vanessa saw the book later, she laughed, because in her world they have a book with the same name, which is a list of medicines. This *Mim's List* was a list of anti-demon devices. It had been read so much that it was practically falling to pieces. I put page twenty-eight back when it fell out and found page thirty-four. Weapons in order of effectiveness. Engraved knife, demon knife, spirit knife, engraved gun—and so on, with notes and drawings after each, right down to sharpened stake. The one at the top of the list was

> LIVING BLADE—deadly to demons of any
> strength on any plane. Said to be a blade
> composed of human spirit. Known only in
> legend, where it is stated that a living blade
> can carve its way through to the Otherworld.
> See Koris Khanssaga 11. 1039–44.

"Yes," I said. "But I don't know if she can do knives."

"Ask her!" Konstam said feverishly.

So I asked Helen, but she wouldn't even talk to me by then. She just went away and sat in the living room.

Konstam nearly went mad with frustration. He was quite, quite sure, from what Joris had told him, that Helen could carve up that triangular fort, and *Them* inside it, if she wanted. He said that if Helen had been born a Khan, she would have been the most famous demon hunter of all time. I explained that Helen had been quite highly thought of in the House of Uquar too, but her father had called her arm a deformity. Konstam cursed Helen's father. He cursed demon-fashion, which is a very startling kind of cursing. Helen probably heard him—he was raging round and round the hall—but she wouldn't speak. Not even the tip of her nose would come out of her hair.

Vanessa went and coaxed Helen. That did no good. So Konstam rounded on me and told me to *do* something.

I had to spend the rest of the afternoon collecting critters. I knew it was the only thing to do. I found a toad and a slug and half a hundred earwigs, and I put them on the living-room carpet in front of Helen. Vanessa said her mother would have fits if she knew. A waste of fits, since Helen didn't even look at them. Then Adam came out of his sulk—he was beginning to be able to sit down by then—and told me there were rats in the shed where Vanessa kept her unpoetic car. They used to be his, he said, but they got out.

So I took a handful of cheese to the shed and stalked rats for an hour. I got one too. A fat black beauty, which bit like a demon. I carried it wriggling and twisting into the living room and held it out to Helen. Her hands came out and clasped it lovingly. She put it on her knee, and the rat went all woffly and cuddly and obliging. Its whiskers shimmered happily. A small noise came from behind Helen's hair.

"What's that?" I said unwisely.

Helen's hair flung back. I got the full ready-to-bite treatment. *"I said thank you!"* Helen yelled. She was furious. I got out quick.

Vanessa was just putting stuff on my rat bites when there was a crisis in the kitchen again. The knives I'd bought were no ruddy good. The idea had been to sharpen them up and turn them into demon weapons by engraving the right signs on the blades and hilts. But it turned out that the things knives were made of in this world were not strong enough to stand the signs. Plastic handles melted under Shen. They got Shen to go on most of the blades, but any other signs just crumbled the metal away.

"Jamie!" Konstam shouted. The errand boy came running.

I was to go with Joris, Konstam said, because Joris knew good demon steel when he saw it, and we were to get the best knives we could of that kind, with handles of wood only, or pure bone. So off we trotted.

Well, I said Joris was touchy. He was worse than that. He made such a fuss over those knives that

I would have hit him if he hadn't been twice as strong as me. I got really annoyed, because he drew so much attention to us in the shops. He'd consented to put on Dr. Macready's old raincoat over his demon hunter's outfit—because Konstam told him to—but he would wear it open. People noticed him because of all the fuss he made. Then they stared at the black sign on his chest and asked him if he was a judo expert. Someone else said did he swallow swords?

"Joris," I said, when we finally came away with a bundle of knives, "I've had a hard day. And I don't think you're quite your old sunny self. In fact, I warn you, you'll have *Them* deciding you've entered play here, if you go on at this rate. Remember you're still a Homeward Bounder until you get Home."

Joris stopped walking. He kicked a tin can that happened to be lying there. The clatter made quite a lot of people turn round and stare. Since it was late on a Saturday afternoon, there were crowds of people about. I swear Joris waited until as many people as possible were turned to look at us. Then he shouted out, *"I hate being a slave!"*

Luckily, nobody thought he meant just that. They didn't have such things in that world. A lot of people turned away in embarrassment. I tried to make Joris move on. "But I thought you liked Konstam."

"Oh yes, I like Konstam." Joris consented to shamble gloomily on. "I love demon hunting. I'd never want to do anything else, or work with anyone but Konstam. It's just being a slave I hate."

"Oh," I said. "How long have you hated it?" It seemed to me that it could only have been half an hour at the longest. But no.

"Ever since I was first sold," Joris said miserably. "Only you don't think about it. It doesn't do any good. I suppose I started to think about hating it when I thought I wasn't going to see Konstam again. Then Adam wanted to sell Vanessa. That made me feel terrible." Then he stood still again and shouted. *"I hate it!"* And we had an audience again.

"Do keep walking," I said. "Look, if you hate it that much, why don't you tell Konstam? He doesn't seem the kind of man who—"

"What good would that do?" Joris demanded, in a sort of half-shout. "The only way to stop being a slave is to buy my freedom, and slaves aren't allowed to earn money. And even if I *could* earn money, where am I going to get anything like twenty thousand crowns from?"

"Um," I said. "I see your problem. Wait a moment! You demon hunters are the only people I know who can get into other worlds. What's—"

Someone called out, "Can't you find somewhere else to rehearse your play?"

That made Joris move on fast.

"What's to stop you," I panted, as I pattered along beside him, "putting money away in a bank somewhere like this world, where they don't have slaves?"

"That's a good idea," Joris said, striding along. "But I'd have to tell Konstam—Oh no! I'd just *never* earn all that money. It's hopeless."

There didn't seem to be anything I could say to cheer him up, either.

We got back to the house. There was Helen, and there was Konstam with her. They were standing in the hall, just in front of Fred, both looking delighted. Helen's face was all pink through the brown, just like Konstam's. Helen had her sleeve rolled up and her arm was—well, it almost wasn't. It was like an arm-shaped bar of light. I could see the carpet and Fred through it. But the odd thing about it—the really creepy thing—was that in the arm, in the middle of the bar of light, I could see the faint, faint outline of another arm, a much smaller arm, all drawn up and withered. That was the arm Helen had been born with. No wonder she hadn't wanted to show anyone.

Konstam looked up at us like the cat that had the cream. "Look! We have our living blade!"

You know, I almost stormed off in a sulk. I do all the work, and Konstam reaps the benefit! But that would have been behaving like Adam. Adam had the cheek to come up to me in the kitchen, looking injured.

"I don't know why Konstam had to be like that when I said I'd sell him Vanessa. It was only a joke."

"Oh yes?" I said. I knew it wasn't a joke. He knew I knew.

I made him help me get supper after that. I felt

like Cinderella, but I didn't feel like being on my own. I kept thinking, I've put off going Home for these people, and none of them have even noticed, let alone thanked me! I thought a good supper might cheer me up. I could cook better than Vanessa, anyway, but, then, almost anyone could.

Adam drifted off, in the most natural, absent-minded way, as soon as I got cooking, and everyone else disappeared as well. Usually people drift back when food is ready. The human race is born with an instinct, I think. But this lot didn't. I had to go and find them. Helen and Adam were poring over the rule books in the basement. The rest of them were in the living room. Joris was shouting in there. I sort of hovered in the doorway, not knowing if I was interrupting or not.

Konstam had his arm round Vanessa. He was a quick worker, was Konstam. Joris was standing in front of them, shouting. He had his most hurt, freckled look. "So now you know how much I hate it!" he yelled.

"Then why didn't you *say* so?" Konstam said. "Listen—"

Konstam kept saying "Listen," but Joris was too worked up to attend. "There's no point in telling people, least of all you!" Joris said. "There's no way I could earn any money, is there? There's no way—"

"Joris, *listen* to him!" shouted Vanessa.

She made it a real scream. That got through to Joris. He came to and blinked at her.

"I keep trying to tell you," Konstam said. "I'd have explained years ago if I'd known you were this worried. As far as I'm concerned, you're as free as I am, in this world or any other, except our own. You're only a slave there because the law doesn't allow you to be freed until you're eighteen. But Elsa Khan has the manumission papers all drawn up ready, and she'll register them the day you're eighteen. Does that make you feel better?"

"No," said Joris. "You've spent a lot of money for nothing."

Konstam laughed. "Nothing, you say? Joris, since you've been my partner, we've earned what you cost twice a year, and sometimes more. Your share is in a special account, waiting until you're eighteen—and before you say what you've opened your mouth to say, yes, you can pay me back if you want to. You'll still be rich even when you have."

Since Joris was looking so flabbergasted, I thought the kindest thing to do was to come in like a butler and bow. "Sirs and madam, supper is served."

XIII

My jabbering machine has decided this is Chapter Thirteen. Very appropriate. Now we come to our war against *Them*.

It was to have been a dawn offensive, just as if it was a mud-brown war, but we overslept a bit. It was quite daft of us, considering the Bounds might have called us any time, but we forgot all about that.

We were talking until late in the night. I'd stopped feeling like Cinderella hours before we went to bed. It was such fun, talking. Homeward Bounders are usually careful not to get too thick with people, but I got careless there. I was really fond of them all. I was even fond of Adam, which Vanessa said was quite difficult to do. But I admired Adam's cool cheek. And I admired the way that he was still joining in the war, even though he couldn't see *Them*. It was like a blind man going to war. I swore to him I'd keep beside him and tell him where *They* were.

It was about the middle of the morning when we were all ready to go. By that time, I'd almost forgotten the Bounds. We had quite a lot of stuff to put on ourselves. It all seemed to me a bit silly—like the charms and amulets ignorant people wear in savage worlds—but Joris swore to me the things worked. I'd taken to believing Joris lately.

For a start, we all wore white somewhere, even Helen, though her white was only the background to the black sign of Shen on her chest. She said, "The Hands of Uquar are always in black." Konstam said he wasn't going to alter that. Helen had her own power and must use it in her own way. But Adam had more nerve than the rest of us, and he asked her why they wore black. Instead of biting him, Helen said, "Didn't I say? It's in mourning for the terrible fate of Uquar."

Adam lent me a white shirt, and he wore the clothes he had worn to play that game in. Vanessa had what she called a white boiler suit. She had even found white boots. When the sign of Shen was fixed to the front of the boiler suit, she looked almost like a demon hunter too. Konstam was enchanted with the way she looked. He held both her hands and told her so.

"Billing and cooing!" Adam said disgustedly.

"Shut up, toad," said Vanessa.

After that, we took the objects with odd names off Frederick M. Allington and hung them round our necks or strapped them on our wrists as Konstam told us. Adam said Fred looked a little naked now. He fetched a newspaper that had arrived on the doormat and gave it to Fred to hold under his bony arm.

"It's the thirteenth today," he said, and showed me the paper. It was Sunday July 13th. "I hope that's an omen for *Them*."

"You don't talk of omens," Konstam said severely. "Here is a knife each. Are we ready to go now?"

We were ready. Vanessa and Adam had both written letters to their parents—they told the exact truth in them and explained all about *Them*, even though I'd tried to persuade them not to. Vanessa put her letter on the hall table. Adam put his between Fred's teeth. Then we got into the unpoetic car, with a lot of squeezing, and drove to *Their* fort again.

Third time lucky, I kept telling myself nervously, while we were creeping in the uncanny silence among the bushes. The silence really got me, while we were crossing the dip and making for the other side of the fort, where the door must be. I kept looking at Joris to encourage myself. Joris was so happy after what Konstam had told him that he was smiling even now.

We got to the gravel terrace on that side of the triangular building. And there was the door. It seemed to be plate-glass, with a handle in it. I could see the canal arches reflected in it. Konstam had said there was no point being secret, so we came boldly out of the bushes and crossed the gravel to the door. I could see all our white-clothed reflections in it as we came. I didn't blame Adam for only seeing those reflections. I could barely see *Them* beyond. And that was not right. It was different from the way I had seen things at the Old Fort. *They* had both turned to look at us. *They* seemed to be smiling.

"*They* knew we were coming," I said.

"Of course," said Konstam. He put his white glove firmly on the door handle. "It stands to reason *They* know. Adam and Vanessa must show on *Their* table. I must be missing from mine." He jerked the handle.

I had a moment of pure panic. "Then—"

"I'm relying on you three random factors," said Konstam. I told you Konstam was brave. Nothing would have possessed me to go there, if I'd realized *They*'d know. "This door is shut. Helen."

Helen came forward, rolling up her sleeve, and her arm turned to a bar of light as she did it. Behind the glass, *They* looked uneasily at one another and moved back.

"Now *They*'re worried," said Konstam. "I thought *They* would be."

Helen stretched our her bar of light—it still worked like an arm—and touched the glass of the door. The glass shriveled and writhed like hot cellophane. Cracks spread out in it from Helen's near invisible fingers. Then it was not there any more. There was just a dim space. Konstam leaped into this space with a ringing shout, and Joris and Helen followed him. As Vanessa went through, I took

Adam's arm to lead him after, but he pushed me off.

"It's all right. I can see *Them* now." And he took his glasses off as if it was more comfortable not seeing *Them* too well.

Inside, *They* were retreating down the triangular room, hurriedly from Konstam and very, very warily from Helen. Joris was in front of the massive door at the other end, ahead of *Them*. Adam, Vanessa and I spread out on either side of the machines, to make sure *They* didn't try to get away this end. By that time, Konstam and Helen were going round either end of the table, under the great hanging dice. *They* seemed to be trapped.

I couldn't resist taking a look at the table. It was amazing. It didn't seem big enough to hold all it did—but there it all was, everything in the world, down to the tiniest detail. Whatever you looked at, you saw clear, clear, and very small. I saw a mud-brown war going on somewhere in Africa, and another in the north of India. I saw a yacht capsize in an ocean. I saw the very city we were in, with tiny cars and minute people going about their Sunday business. You could see into churches and cars and houses if you wanted, although they all had roofs—I don't know how that was done. I even saw a tiny black triangle where we should have been ourselves. But that was the one thing you couldn't see into.

I only glanced for a second. When I looked up again, the room was one of many triangular rooms. There were rooms all round, and above and beyond and below, just as I had seen them before. Only this time, *They* were not strolling over for a look. *They* were hurrying towards us urgently.

"Oh my Gawd!" said Adam.

There was an awful noise. It was inhuman. I couldn't tell whether it was a hooter or a bell—it was something like both, and quite deafening. While it was sounding, the triangles were all melting and moving and expanding. You felt as if you were tipping all ways at once. It made me dizzy. And it happened in no time at all. When it had finished, we were in what I'm now sure is the *real* Real Place. It was the one Joris had seen. A vast, vast hall stretched not-quite-seeably as far as we could tell in any direction, with tables and tables and tables, and dice, and multitudes of machines. And *They* were there in multitudes too, closing swiftly in on us, horrible and hard-to-see, in a host of gray cloaks.

It all happened so quickly, that was the trouble. "Back to back!" Konstam shouted. Joris was already gone by then, among gray cloaks. Helen yelled something in another language and ran at *Them*. The beam of light that her arm cast in here whirled across a gray group of *Them*. I saw *Their* faces in it clearly for the first time. I don't want to talk about that. They were too horrible.

Then Helen was gone. She was not swallowed up or anything. She just wasn't there. Konstam grabbed for Vanessa, but she was gone. Then Konstam was. I looked round for Adam, but he wasn't there either. Then I went berserk. I turned round, and there was one of *Them* just behind me. I went at him with my demon knife. He went backwards very hurriedly. All I got was his cloak. Then *They* were all round me, and I was sort of hurled aside. *They* weren't gentle. I landed with the most awful bang and cracked my head on something.

When I had finished rolling about—I was not quite knocked silly, but not really there either—I sat up on grass. It was the same kind of mild, doubtful sunlight that we had set off to war in. The thing that I had cracked my head on was a little white statue of a man in chains. I glowered at it. It was so stupidly artistic—not like the real thing at all.

The first thing I thought was: I'm Home!

Then I thought: No I'm not. This is Adam's world. But none of it has happened.

Then I knew it *had* happened, and I got up— using the statue's head to help me—and looked round. Sure enough, I was down in the dip of a small triangular garden or park. There were bushes uphill all round me, a pink fort-like building half hidden up ahead, and the arches of a canal marching across the sky at one side. And I was quite alone. Somehow, I'd hoped that at least one of the others would have been slung here with me. But I could see it made sense to split us up.

At that, I felt terrible. My throat ached, and I could hardly see the canal arches when I turned that way. I knew that there was hardly one chance in a million that I would run into any of the others again. The Bounds are boundlessly huge. I was back in Adam's world all right. I squeezed my eyes shut, and when I opened them again I could see it was Adam's world from the fancy yellow brickwork of the canal arches. Where the rest of them were, *They* alone knew. But it looked to me that Vanessa's theory about overloading the Bounds didn't work. Because I knew, as sure as I knew I stood there in Adam's world, that the rest of my friends were scattered far and wide as Homeward Bounders. *They* couldn't kill any of us with all that demon protection. *They* hadn't been able to kill Joris. So it followed that we all had to be discards.

Then I thought I'd check up on *Them*. *They* obviously didn't care that I was wandering about in *Their* park. So I said to myself that I didn't care about *Them* either. And I went up among the bushes and crunched out on the gravel and took a look at the door. It was back again. It looked just like glass. But I didn't think it was glass. *They* were behind it. *They* looked rather tense when *They* saw me. *They* didn't pretend to be busy. *They* stood together and stared.

I wanted *Them* to know I didn't care. I still had my demon knife in my hand. Just to show *Them*, I slashed at the pink granite of the building, beside the door. I think there was a deal of virtue in those signs Konstam had put on the knife. You can't usually carve granite with a knife. But this knife made a nice deep mark. So I slashed away until I had carved out that sign I had never seen, the rarest one of all. A joke. It said: YOU CAN TELL *THEM* YOU'RE A HOMEWARD BOUNDER. Inside, *They* seemed to relax when *They* saw that was all I was doing. That annoyed me. I didn't see what *They* had to be scared of in me, but I didn't mind *Them* being scared. I looked at the sign. It was not so unlike Shen. I squinted down at Shen on my chest to make sure. It only needed two more strokes to *be* Shen. So I put those two strokes in. The knife broke on the last one, so I threw it down and went away. I didn't care how *They* felt any longer.

It was hard work getting over the wall. It made my arm hurt a lot. But I got over and went up along the side street. There was Vanessa's unpoetic car parked at the top of the street. That would stay there until they did whatever they did with leftover cars. Vanessa wouldn't be back for some time—if ever. I went round the corner to the front of the pink granite building. No harpoons. But there were broken off ends of railings along the wall in front. I went and looked at the front door. There was a plate on this one too. It didn't say as much as the one I had remembered. Just THE OLD FORT and a crowned anchor underneath.

"I suppose *They* call them all Old Forts," I said, and I went away, uphill through the empty shopping center. Funny—in every world I've known, when a place is empty there is always paper blowing about. A depressing fact.

I didn't know where I was going—but I sort of did, if you know what I mean. The cold foot ache was beginning to gather in my chest, worse than I had ever known it. I suppose I knew, even then. I went on and up, through a pattern of streets that I knew from Home, past buildings I had never seen before. And at last I was in a part where the pattern was awfully, dreadfully, drearily familiar. And I thought: Do I want to go on? And I did want to. I went round a corner and up a short hill and came to a school. It was exactly where my old school, Churt House, would have been, but it was nearly quite different.

There was a lot more of this school. It was behind a long railing. Most of it was the square new kind of building Adam's world seemed to go in for, with lots of windows. But I went along to a high gate made of bars, with a painted shield fixed to the bars. The design on the shield was the same as the badge on Adam's blazer. And I peered through the gate, among the new buildings. One building in the midst of them was older, and small and chapel-shaped. I knew that building all right—though not as well as I had thought. I stepped back and looked at the gate again to be sure. The school's name was on a board by the gate. It said:

**QUEEN ELIZABETH ACADEMY
(formerly CHURT HOUSE)**

Then I knew, really. But there was something else I had to make sure of first. I went on, still uphill, to the street with trees and broad pavements, where Ahasuerus had been asleep, and up the alley where Joris's knife had got me. There was still a little dark patch of my blood there.

Adam's house was fourth along of the big pleasant houses in the street above the alley. I went into the drive. The trees hid the house. I didn't notice until I was right up to the house that there was an extremely nice-looking car outside the front door. Really that car was almost poetic. Beyond it, the front door was open.

Oh well, I thought. There'll be someone to ask. And I ought to explain to their parents anyway.

I didn't ring the doorbell. I just went straight in. Both parents were there. She was standing in the kitchen doorway, in the good light, reading Vanessa's letter. She was a nice-looking fussy lady who wore glasses. He was standing by Fred, reading Adam's letter. He was a tall man, thick-built, and he wore a little beard. Both of them were still and hushed with worry. While I stood there, the big black rat I'd caught for Helen yesterday went scampering across the hall. *She* looked at it, watched it scamper, and didn't really notice it. That was how worried she was. She was the kind who would have torn the place apart over that rat in the ordinary way.

I decided not to bother her. *He* was the one I needed to ask anyway. He had already looked up and seen me. I don't know if he saw the rat at all.

"Are you Dr. Macready?" I said.

"Yes, I am," he said. He noticed nothing but my size at first. "I'm afraid Adam's not here at the moment," he said.

"I know he isn't," I said. "I came to ask you something."

He made himself look at me a little more at that. And, as he looked, I could see him trying to collect his doctordom. It was like someone trying to put on a coat when the sleeves are inside out. He couldn't really get into being a doctor, but he did his best. "About that arm?" he said. "I'm not really on call at the moment, you know. You'd better take it down to Casualty at the Royal Free."

I looked at my arm. Blood was oozing through the shirt Adam had lent me. Not surprising. "I didn't come about that," I said.

He went on trying to get into being a doctor. He really tried. "Playing a dressing-up game, were you?" he said. He had seen Shen on my chest. "And it went and got rough, I suppose."

I began to wonder if he'd ever listen to me. "See here," I said. "I just came to ask you a couple of questions. When you've answered them, I'll go. I know you don't want to be bothered with me just now."

That made him look at me in a different way. Being a doctor, I suppose he was used to dealing with people in funny states of mind. Anyway, he could see I was in at least as bad a way as he was.

"What do you want to know?" he said cautiously.

"Your grandmother," I said. "The lady doctor. You've an album in there with pictures of her. What was her name?"

"Elsie," he said. "Elsie Hamilton Macready."

So it *was* Elsie. I would have liked to ask how she came by the expensive shoes, but I let that pass. Elsie could get hold of anything she set her mind on. "She must have married one of the Macready boys in the next court," I said. "We used to play football with them. Which one was it? The eldest—John—or the other one—Will?"

"No, no. It was Graham," he said, staring at me. "The youngest."

"Graham!" I said. "I hardly *knew* Graham! He was no good at football at all. He read books all the time." But he was Elsie's age, come to think of it. "Do you know about the rest of Elsie's family?" I asked. "Her brothers. She had two brothers."

Now he was really staring. "Robert went to Australia," he said. "The elder one, James, disappeared when he was a boy. They dragged the canal for him."

And now you're going to do it for Adam, I thought. I ought to have gone then. He was staring at me as if I were Fred suddenly come to life and speaking. Which I was in a way. She was beginning to stare too. "Two more things," I said. "What's that game people dress up in white for?"

"Eh?" he said. "You mean cricket?"

"Oh," I said. I'd heard of the game, of course. "Cricket! That really foxed me, not knowing it was cricket. We only played football. I thought you played cricket in shiny top hats, with a bent sort of bat."

"They certainly used to," he said. "But that was *over* a hundred years ago."

"It's no good accusing me of fraud," I said. I was past caring. "That really is all I know of cricket. I only got firsthand knowledge two days ago. One last thing. Do you mind taking that newspaper from under Fred's arm and reading me out the date on it?"

He looked at me sidewise, but he took out the paper and he read out the date on it, just as I remembered it from earlier that morning. "July the thirteenth, nineteen-eighty."

"Thanks," I said. My voice was dithering about. I could hardly speak. "Then it *is* over a hundred years. When I was last here, it was eighteen seventy-nine."

Then I turned round and went away. I didn't want to be a living Fred to them. I went quite fast, but he came after me. Beard and all, he was not so unlike my father, and my father would have run after his great-uncle too. "Hey!" he shouted. "Let me see to that arm anyway!" Which shows he understood.

"No thanks," I shouted. "You've got one Fred!" Then I ran and left him standing by his shiny poetic car.

I ran back downhill. I wanted to check up on

that canal. I'd remembered it wrong all these years. And how *many* years was the real shock! I hadn't thought I'd spent a hundred years Homeward Bound. What fooled me was the way time jerks about from world to world. I thought it went on in one place and stayed the same at Home. But I have been on over a hundred worlds, and I suppose it does average out at a year a world. So I suppose it was no wonder that I'd forgotten and things had changed.

But, you see, I hadn't forgotten, not really. The moment I first saw those canal arches, I'd known. But I just wouldn't believe it. I just couldn't believe that even *They* could be such cheats. I'd gone about working overtime not to believe it. I'd noticed all the differences, as hard as I could, and all the time the sameness had been creeping, creeping up on me. I'd known as soon as my head banged that statue that *They* had sent me Home. Except that I wasn't Home. I never could be.

When I was halfway to the canal, the Bounds called.

Wasn't that just like *Them*? *They* crush us in seconds, *They* sling us every which way, *They* make sure I know just what cruel joke *They*'ve been playing all these years—*They* give me just time enough—and then *They* get straight back to *Their* game. There came the well-known dragging and yearning. I stood still and quivered with it.

It was coming from right behind me. I think

it was from those vegetable patches after all. If that was the nearest Boundary, that meant I had quite a way to go. And on Sunday, with no money, in a world with all those rules and regulations, I was going to have a hard time getting there. I turned round to answer the call and start getting there. I didn't mind leaving. Nothing mattered anymore.

Then I stopped. If nothing mattered anymore, then *They* didn't matter either. "Why should I keep on letting you push me about?" I said to *Them*. "I'm going where I want to go for once."

I knew where I wanted to go. And I turned right round again. There was another Boundary much nearer. The Old Fort and the triangular garden must be a Boundary, or Joris's instrument wouldn't have gone mad there. It was sealed off from the city somehow. That was why it was so silent in there. But I knew it was a Boundary, and I was going to use it and go where I wanted and spite *Them*.

The call is hard enough to bear if something stops you answering it. If you turn your back on it on purpose, it gets quite horrible. But I knew it could be done. I'd done it on that cattle-world eighty years ago. And I think all the things Konstam had made me hang round my neck and strap on my wrists helped quite a bit. Konstam knew his job, even if he had underestimated *Them*. Konstam was quite something. I mean, Helen and I got fed up with Joris for talking about Konstam all the time, but it was easy to see why he did. I thought it wouldn't take me long, in my next world, to buttonhole the first Homeward Bounder I met and tell him all about Konstam too. My friend Konstam the demon hunter. Konstam raging round the hall telling me to catch rats for Helen.

The call dragged and tore and choked at me. I had to lean forward to move against it. I remember two or three people I passed staring at me—a boy with a bleeding arm and a black badge on his chest, walking downhill to the canal as if he were climbing Everest. I must have looked odd. But I kept going, thinking of my friends. Joris and Adam and Vanessa. It occurred to me that Vanessa and Konstam had fallen in love. In which case, they must be feeling terrible now. That was why Konstam had spanked Adam, of course—not out of righteous indignation—because Adam's offer tempted him. He probably knew the rest of the Khans wouldn't stand for him owning two slaves.

Then I thought of Helen. That was when I was trying to climb the wall into the garden, and it was really hard work. Helen hiding a withered arm in another arm made of spirit, just like she hid her face in her hair. Helen taking the Archangel out of me and snarling and snapping. She couldn't thank people, Helen. She hated saying thank you. As I said, Helen, my friendly neighborhood enemy. I wasn't likely to be in the same neighborhood as Helen, ever again.

That got me over the wall. And *wham*! The

Bounds called from the other way at once—pulling and yelling and wrenching me towards the green dip in the center of the triangle.

But I didn't answer them even then. I'd taken care to climb the wall as near the Fort as I could get. I shoved through the bushes and crunched across the gravel and glared in through the window at *Them*. *They* left *Their* machines and backed away from me. *They* were really nervous of me. I couldn't see why *They* should be, but I was glad. I made a face at *Them*. It was the only thing left to be glad about.

Then I let myself answer the call at last. It came so hard I had to run, crashing through the bushes and careering down the slope of grass. But at the bottom, I dug my heels in the turf and went slow. I didn't want to whizz straight to the Boundary and crash off just anywhere. There was one particular place I wanted to go. Mind you, I wasn't sure I could get there, but I was determined to try.

So I crept up to that white statue as if I was stalking it. And when I was about a yard away from it, I stopped. I knew the Boundary must be just beside it. I leaned forward, very, very carefully, and I laid hold of one of those amazing carved stone chains hanging on the statue. When I had hold of it, I pulled myself towards the statue with it, gently, gently, and all the time I thought hard of the person the statue was really of. Him chained to his rock.

XIV

And I did it. A very severe twitch happened.

He was really surprised to see me. He had been sort of hanging backwards, the way he was before, with his head tipped further back and his eyes shut. When I landed on his ledge his eyes shot open and he jumped—really jumped. He may not have been human, but he had feelings just like I did. And he was astonished.

"I didn't expect to see you again," he said, and he carefully dragged a loop of massive teardrop chain away from just beside me. I could have touched it and been gone again the next second.

It seemed to me that his voice had trembled a bit. It was more than astonishment. He was ten times lonelier than I was. I took a careful look at him. His wound was no worse than before, which is not saying much, and his clothes were perhaps a bit more ragged. He had made a bit of progress with the red beard he seemed to be growing, but that was all. He hadn't changed any more than I had. He was just as cold, and wet all over.

"Yes, you're right out of luck," I said, joking to cheer him up a bit. "One of *Them* tried to make me forget all about you, but unfortunately for you, a dog rattled its chain at me a minute after, and I called you to mind again. I've come to get you another drink of water."

"That's very kind of you," he said, smiling. "But I'm not so thirsty this time. Someone gave me a drink a while ago, and it's raining. I've been drinking the rain."

He was right it was raining. The weather was lousy up there. It was raining in chilly, mizzling gusts that covered us both with little fine drops, like miniatures of those great links of his chains. "Are you sure?" I said.

"Sure," he said.

I sat myself down on the wet rock, leaning against the crag beside him, as near as I could get without touching the chains. There was no fog this time, only driving rain-clouds, but there was not what I'd call much of a view. Nothing but drizzling pink rocks. His rock was turned away from the sea. *They* hadn't even allowed him that much pleasure. While I was thinking that this was not much to look at for all eternity, I noticed that the rocks were the same as the granite the Old Fort was built of. I wondered if *They*'d chosen it for hardness, or for some other reason.

"Who was it gave you a drink?" I said. "Anyone I know?"

"Ahasuerus," he said.

"Oh him," I said. "I met him a couple of days ago. How mad is he?"

"Pretty mad," he said. "He's worse every time he comes here."

Now, I had meant to ask if *They* did anything to stop Ahasuerus coming, and if not, why not. But, somehow, the thought of Ahasuerus set me off. It was just as if I were Joris and someone had mentioned Konstam. Everything seemed to drop away and leave just me. "But he's not quite crazy," I said. "He talked some sense. He knew how it felt. I don't blame him for being crazy after all those years. He talked about hope being a millstone round your neck—and he was right! That's just what it is. You're so busy staggering along hoping, that you can't see the truth. He told me the truth. I was too busy hoping to see it. He said *They* lead you along with hope. And that's just what *They* do! *They* kick you out and set you going from world to world, and *They* promise you that if you can get Home, the rules allow you to stay there. Rules! Utter cheat. *They* knew, as well as I do now, that no one who's a Homeward Bounder can *ever* get Home. It just can't be done."

"What's happened then?" he asked. He was really sorry for me. It always beat me how he could think of anyone else in his situation, but he could.

"What's happened," I said, "is that I've been Home, and it wasn't my Home anymore. I was exactly a hundred years too late for it."

And I told him all that had happened. But you know how you can talk and have other things go through your mind at the same time. While I talked away, I heard myself talking in English, and I saw him nodding, and heard the chains drag when he did, and I knew he understood every word. And I understood when he said things like "And then what?" or laughed about Helen and the rat. Helen had told me she was taught English because it was the right language for the ways of the worlds. I always thought *They* spoke English. But that was another cheat, or maybe another mistake of mine. It was quite another language. It was just that I could understand it as part of being able to see *Them*. And I understood him for the same reason.

I told him about our useless attempt to invade *Their* Real Place. "And all *They* did was sling us straight out again, really," I said. "*They* slung me so that I hit my head on a rotten statue that's supposed to be you, and I sat up and knew I was Home. Only it wasn't Home. It was all changed and gone. And I know *They* did it on purpose. *They* wanted to show me I hadn't got a *hope*!"

"You may be wronging *Them* there," he said.

"Don't you try to be fair to *Them*," I said. "Even you can't."

"All I meant was that *They* may have sent you Home," he said, "as a way of stopping you bothering *Them*."

"No," I said. "*They* had the Bounds call me right after that. I'm still a Homeward Bounder. Only I'm not Bound to any Home. I'm just bound the way you are. I can see that now."

There was a bit of a silence. The cold rain made little pittering sounds, and the wind sighed. Then he shifted in his chains, sort of cautiously. I didn't blame him for being restive. He must have ached all over.

"Perhaps you could fetch me a drink, after all," he said.

I got up at once and started edging past the chains. I was glad he'd asked, since it was what I'd come here for. As I shuffled sideways past him, it did strike me that he was standing differently, standing not leaning, but I thought nothing of it. He had to ease his bones somehow.

I got to the place where I had to climb over the chains because they were hooked up on the anchor. I stopped to look at that anchor. I could have sworn it was rustier than last time.

"You can put your hand on the anchor," he said, "when you climb over. As long as you don't touch the chains." There was a sort of edge to his voice as he said that, which I didn't understand. It was almost as if he was nervous.

He's keener for a drink than he'll say, I thought. I wished he had let me get him one straightaway. And I put my hand on the big pointed fluke of the anchor, ready to hoist a leg over the chains.

It was a wonder I didn't pitch forward onto my

face. There was a sort of trembling to everything, right through the rock, combined with a strong sideways twitch. I thought I must have touched a chain after all. But I was still there, holding the fluke of the anchor. And that great sharp piece of iron was sinking and shifting under my hand. It split as it sank, into dozens of pointed orange slivers. You know the way iron goes when it rusts. And that anchor rusted as I touched it—rusted so badly in half a second that it was crumbling away into orange dust and bluish flakes before I could get my hand off it. It didn't stop when I let go of it, either. While I was swaying about to get balanced it went on crumbling and flaking, the ring and the shank too, as well as the fluke.

The ring, being the smallest part, was the first thing to fall away into brown nothing. And, as soon as it did, the whole load of heavy transparent chains came loose and fell on the rock with a rattle. That gave rise to a whole lot more rattling, further along, where he was. I looked round to see him dragging first one arm loose, then the other. And as those chains fell down, he kicked them off his feet too. I stared. I couldn't credit it. I had seen how those staples went deep into the granite.

"What did that?" I said.

The trembling had stopped by then. He was standing panting a bit, with one arm up to nurse his wound. "You did," he said. He laughed a little. "I hope you don't think you've been tricked by me now," he said. "I couldn't be quite honest with you. If I had, you might have started hoping again."

"Is that so bad?" I said. "I thought it wasn't good to lose hope."

"The way *They* use hope," he said, "the sooner you lose it the better. Shall we get out of this place?"

"Suits me," I said. "You must hate it a lot more than I do."

We went down the way the stream went down, where the rocks were in jumbled stages. I'd forgotten how big he was. If he hadn't been weak and having to go slow with his wound, I'd never have kept up with him. He kept having to wait for me as it was, and he even had to help me over one or two steep places.

We got down in the end. It was a whole lot warmer down there. While we were walking to the entrance of a valley I could see further along, the rain stopped and the sky turned a misty blue.

"This used to be my Home," he said, as we came into the valley.

It was really peculiar. It ought to have been one of the most beautiful places you ever saw. It was a long, winding valley, with the stream rushing through it and spraying among rocks. Every kind of tree was growing there, in woods up the sides and in clumps by the stream. But it all seemed faded. It wasn't faded the way things fade in autumn. It was more the way an old photograph goes, sort of faint and bleached. The grass wasn't green enough and the rocks were pale. The trees, though they had faded a bit like autumn, into yellowish and pinkish colors, were pale too, and they drooped a bit. Any birds that were singing made a slender sort of sound, as if they were too weak to raise their voices.

He sighed when he saw it. But I noticed that, as we walked along by the stream, color seemed to be draining back into the place. The sky turned bluer. The stream dashed along sharper, and seemed to nourish the grass to a better green. The trees recovered and lifted their leaves up. By the time we came to a white kind of house above the stream in a turn of the valley, everywhere was pretty beautiful, in a gentle sort of way, and the birds were singing their heads off.

There were loaded fruit trees round the house. I helped him pick fruits off them as we went up to the house—there were oranges, apples, pears and big yellow things like living custard. All the while, the valley seemed to be getting brighter and brighter. I saw, while he was reaching up into a tree, that his wound was quite a bit better. So was my arm, when I came to consider it. We took the fruit to the house. Most of the house was a sort of arched porch held up on pillars, where the sun came in good and warm, but there were rooms at the back and up on top.

The first thing he did was to go to the back room and bring out a basket for the fruit and a big kettle. "Eat what fruit you want," he said. "We both need a wash and a warm drink, I think. Will you lay some wood for a fire while I get the water. There should be wood round the side of the house."

There was a sort of hearth-place in the center of the porch, with the old sketchy remains of ash in it. Round the side of the house, the stacked logs and kindling were a bit greenish, but they didn't look as if they had been waiting forever and a day, as I knew they had. I brought a few loads into the porch—my arm was healing the whole time, and the rat bites on my fingers had almost gone by then—and by the time I'd got a fire laid and was looking round for some way to light it, he was back with the water.

"Ah," he said, and knelt down and lit the fire. As he fetched a stand to go over the fire and put the kettle on it, he was laughing. His wound was doing even better than my arm. "It makes me laugh," he said. "*They* put it about on most worlds that I was punished for lighting fires. I think only the world of Uquar knows even half the truth."

"Helen's world?" I said.

"Yes," he said. "If you'd talked much about me to Helen, neither of us would be here now."

It was good to sit by the leaping fire, warm in the sun too. We ate fruit while we waited for the kettle to boil. But I was too nervous to enjoy it at first. "What will *They* do? Won't *They* know you're free?" I said.

"There's nothing *They* can do," he said. "There's no hurry. All *They* can do is hope. *They*'re bound to hope, I'm afraid."

I couldn't help noticing the way he said "bound to hope." It seemed to sum everything up. "Do you think you could explain a bit?" I asked him.

He pushed a lump of custard-fruit into his mouth and wiped his hands on his rags. "Of course," he said. "You have been to *Their* Real Place. You know the ways of the worlds. You have talked of the worlds as being like many reflections in a place of glass. You know almost what I discovered in the beginning. Except," he said, "when I discovered all this, each world was its own Real Place. They still seem that way to those who are not Homeward Bound. But they aren't, not now, and that is my fault." He stared into the flames licking round the logs for a while, sitting with his arms wrapped round his knees and the marks of the chains still on them. "I deserved to be punished," he said. "I saw that a place is less real if it is seen from outside, or only seen in memory; and also that if a person settles in a place and calls that place Home, then it becomes very real indeed. You saw how this valley faded because I had not been in it for a very long time. Well, it came to me that if reality were removed from the worlds, it could be concentrated in one place. And reality could be removed if someone to whom all the worlds were Home never went to any world, but only remembered them. And I mentioned this idea casually to some of *Them*."

"What happened then?" I said.

"Then," he said, "*They* went away and thought.

They are not fools, even if *They* never make discoveries for *Themselves*. *They* saw *They* could use this discovery, just as *They* have since used machines and inventions made by men. After a while, *They* came back and *They* said, 'We want to test this theory of yours. We want you to be the one who remembers the worlds.' And I saw my mistake. I said, 'Give me time to think,' and I hastened away and began to explain my idea to mankind. It was difficult, because not all men were ready to believe me. But I persuaded the people on the world of Uquar to listen, and I had already taught them a great deal when *They* came after me. There were no rules in those days. *They* were stronger than me. *They* brought me back here and *They* chained me as you saw me, and *They* said, 'Don't be afraid. This isn't going to be forever. It's important you know that. We just want to know if what you said is true.' And I said, 'But it is true. There's no need to chain me.' And *They* said, 'But there is a need. If you are chained, there will eventually be someone for whom no place is real, and he will come along and release you. And you are bound to hope that he will come.' And of course that was true too. So *They* went away and left the vulture to remind me."

I looked at his wound, which was now only a nasty red cut. "*They*'d no call to set that vulture on you," I said. "That was an optional extra, if you like!"

"No it wasn't," he said. "It was a reminder, like the anchor. Without the vulture, I might have fallen into apathy and stopped hoping. Hope was what kept me there, you see. Hope is the forward-looking part of memory. My name means Foresight, did you know? And I think *They* found that humorous. *They* knew that as long as I had hope that you would come along, I couldn't free myself. As long as I had hope, *They* could keep *Their* Real Place and play with unreal worlds. I couldn't even hope that I would give up hoping, because that was still hope. And when you came a second time, I hardly dared speak, I was so full of hope. I dared not let you know."

"No wonder you sounded so strung up," I said.

The kettle began to boil then, lifting its lid and chiming it back down again in clouds of steam.

"Good. We can wash," he said. "But let's have a hot drink first. Then I shall put on some proper clothes. But I'm afraid I haven't any clothes to fit you."

"It's all right," I said. "I'm about dry. Besides—" I flipped at my shirt where Vanessa had sewn on the painted sign of Shen—"I'm attached to this. And I reckon it's good protection against *Them.*"

He had got up to shake some kind of herbs into two cups he had ready. He was behaving all the time now as if he had never been chained to that rock— perfectly healthy. He must have been strong. And he stopped and looked at me under his hand that was holding the jar, sort of humorously. "You don't need that," he said. "You don't need anything. No Homeward Bounder does."

"How's that?" I said. "Would you mind explaining?"

He tore a piece off his trousers and used it as a kettle-holder to pour the boiling water on the herbs. Then he handed me a cup. "Careful. It's very hot," he said, and sat back, sipping at his cup. The stuff looked to revive him more. His face seemed to fill out, and that seemed to have an effect on the valley around us too. By then, it was the most beautiful place I had ever seen. "The no interference rule," he said. "You mentioned it to me yourself. Rule Two."

I said, "Do you mean *Them*—" Grammar! my mother would have said—"*They* are bound to keep that rule too?"

"Yes," he said. "If you play a game, then you have to keep the rules, or there is no game anymore. From your account, *They* have been very careful to keep that one."

"Haven't *They* just!" I said furiously. "*They* only robbed me of my Home and my friends and a proper lifetime! That's all!"

"*They* certainly did," he said, and he began looking very sorry for me again. "Drink your drink. It's better hot."

I sipped at the stuff. It was pretty scalding. It was thin and sour and herby and it ought to have tasted awful, but it didn't. It was some of the best stuff I have ever drunk. It cleared my head—or it may have put a few ideas into my head, I don't know—but I know that as I sipped and he talked, I began to understand more and more. Adam had got most of it right about us Homeward Bounders, but there was more to it than we had thought.

"*They* need you Homeward Bounders," he said. "It's not just because *They* enjoy playing dangerously—*They* have to play it that way. You see, even when worlds are Real Places, they have a way of multiplying—splitting off and making new worlds—and they do it even more when they're drained of reality. *They* like that. It means more of *Them* can play. But, after a while, there were so many new worlds that *They* were playing with numbers that I hadn't known. So I couldn't keep these new worlds from becoming dangerously real. *They* found *They* had to have people to keep these worlds unreal for *Them*. *They* did it by promising you all a Real Place and making sure you never found it. Home."

"So hope did the same for us as it did for you!" I said. "But I still don't see why it was me that rusted the anchor. Couldn't Ahasuerus have done it for you? Or the Flying Dutchman? They both said they hadn't a hope."

"They knew they hadn't a hope of getting Home," he said. "But they did have hope. *They* took care to tell them that someone was bound to release me. It was only towards the end, when the number of Homeward Bounders was almost complete, that *They* had to stop telling people that. Otherwise I would have given up hope."

"There has to be a reason," I said, "for the

numbers of us being limited. Why is that?"

"It has to be no more than the numbers of *Them*," he said. "You are very dangerous to *Them* anyway, because of Rule Two. For, as you pointed out, *They* have injured you and interfered with you considerably. If all Homeward Bounders got together and realized this, it would go hard with *Them*. But if there is even one more—"

"I get you!" I said. "Then we tip the balance of reality our way, and the reality drains out of *Their* Real Place. And there are several more now!"

"That," he said, "was why *They* sent you Home, I think."

"Oh no," I said. "The Bounds called—" And then I stopped, because I realized I was still trying to hide the truth from myself, just like I had in Adam's world. What had happened there was that I had already seen that I was still going to have to walk the Bounds, *before* the Bounds called. I had, in a way, chosen to stay a Homeward Bounder. Not that there was much choice. "I think," I said slowly, supping the last of my drink, "I may be very dangerous to *Them*. Am I?"

"You are," he said. He looked very troubled. "What else do you see?"

"I don't want to think about it yet," I said. "Come on. What are we waiting for? Let's go and finish *Them* off, before *They* think of something *They* can do about it."

He laughed. "We're waiting to rest and wash.

There's nothing *They* can do. *They* can only hope you won't understand."

But of course I did understand—nearly as well as I do now. I sat and had some more of the drink and thought about it, while he went away into the back room to wash. I gave *Them* credit for quick thinking. When we invaded the Real Place, *They* had to get rid of us, and *They* couldn't kill any of us because of all the protection we carried, and three of us were Homeward Bounders anyway. So *They* slung Adam and Vanessa and Joris and Konstam on the Bounds, knowing that Joris and Konstam, being demon hunters, could get Home quite easily. *They* slung Helen too, because, with her Hand of Uquar, she was a real menace to *Them*. But *They* had to send me Home, because, even when Joris and Konstam got Home, I would overload the Bounds. *They* thought I was the most harmless one. But then I went and chose to go on being a Homeward Bounder, and that made me Real. It made me like the joker in a pack of cards. No wonder *They* were scared of me!

About this time, he came out of the back room clean and shaved and wearing clothes that put me in mind of Joris's uniform. "Your turn to wash," he said.

"Do you come from the demon hunter's world?" I said.

"No," he said. "I come from yours. I'm the last of a race called Titans."

"And where do *They* come from?" I said.

"You find *Them* on every world," he said. "But the chief among *Them* came from the world of demons."

"That fits," I said. I got up to wash. "I'd better make an early call there then." I didn't look at him as I went. I knew he understood, and I think it upset him.

We set off to the proper battle as soon as I was ready.

He didn't bother with Boundaries. He was demon-kin that way. And anyone with him didn't need Boundaries either. We were off at the edge of things where his Home was, and at first the worlds were pretty scattered. It was like walking on stepping-stones—if you can imagine nothingness between each stone, and the stepping-stones themselves being all round you, instead of just under your feet. Then, when the worlds were closer together, it was more like walking down a corridor, lined with different skies overhead; and for walls, cities, fields, mountains and oceans, all flicking by as we walked.

I still don't know what called the Homeward Bounders. He may have done. But I think it was more likely that we had made a move in *Their* games, walking as we did, that canceled all the other moves and called the Homeward Bounders to us. Anyway, they kept appearing, more and more of them, and came with us in a crowd as we went. I didn't see anyone I knew. There were so many.

I suppose making *Their* kind of move meant that we were keeping *Their* time. Maybe we were up to a week on the way, but it didn't feel like it. It seemed only like half an hour or so before we got to a part where worlds were so thick about us that they weren't like a corridor any more, but really like reflections all round a place of glass. I kept peering for the Real Place inside and through all the sliding shapes of cities and deserts and skies, but not a sight of it could I get.

"*They*'ve hidden *Themselves*," I said.

"Yes," he said. "But not well enough. Someone has marked *Them* out."

He pointed. And glimmering through the shifting worlds like a small far-off star I saw the sign of Shen.

"Oh," I said. "That was me. I didn't know it would show up so."

We sort of clove our way towards that star-sign, bringing the other Homeward Bounders with us, until Shen was hanging just in front of us. All we could see was Shen and our own many selves reflected beside it.

"How are we going to get in at *Them*?" I said.

"You can go in," he said. "But we need your friend Helen to let in the rest of us."

I turned to the nearest ones in the crowd. "Give a shout for Helen Haras-uquara, will you?" I said. "She must be here somewhere." Actually, a lot of us were late, having the usual trouble getting to the

Bounds. I was lucky that Helen was there. She was at the back of the crowd. They pushed and jostled her through to us.

She had got a new hairstyle. Most of her hair was pushed back in a ribbon. Just one hank fell down in front, right down the middle of her face. But she even pushed that away when she saw me.

"Jamie!" she shrieked. But then she saw him standing huge beside me, and she knelt down. That astonished me. I never thought to see Helen kneel to anyone. "You are called Uquar," she said. "We have a statue of you in chains in the House of Uquar. They say your bonds are our Bounds, and you were bound for telling us the ways of the worlds. They say only one without hope can undo them."

"That's right," he said. "Jamie undid them. Helen, get up and use the Hand of Uquar for us. We must get in there and destroy as many of *Them* as we can." And he called to the rest of the crowd, "When we get in, each of you is allowed to destroy one of *Them*. That is *Their* rule."

"All right," Helen said, through the cheering this caused. "Only if you make a mess of it too, I'll never forgive you!" She was still Helen, Hand or no Hand.

Helen got up and pulled up her sleeve, and the light of that weird arm shone on the surface of the Real Place. I tried not to look at that other withered little arm inside it. And, in fact, there wasn't time to look, because so many things happened then. The surface of the Place shriveled and cracked and was gone, just like the glass door of the Old Fort. Only this time there was a huge opening. We were all pushing forward to pour in, when there was a lot of shouting and jerking in the front of the crowd, and a figure in white came leaping out into the opening.

"Wait!" he shouted. It was Konstam. He had not managed to work his way Home yet. "Wait!" he shouted. "*They* are demons. You must kill each of *Them* twice!"

It needed saying, but I don't think everyone heard. I was being pushed through the opening, and Konstam was being pushed away backwards as he shouted, as all the other Homeward Bounders pressed forward to get at *Them*. Most of us shouted, war-cries or insults or just shouts. Not all of us had weapons, but *They* ran away from us whether we did or not.

They took advantage of Konstam's interruption to cheat. *They* always did cheat if *They* could. While he was shouting and we were all pushing in, *They* ran away towards the sides of the Place. As soon as I got in there, it began to get smaller. Its edges weren't out of sight anymore. Pieces sort of dropped off it—and a number of *Them* seized the opportunity to drop off with the pieces. *They* sealed my fate by doing that— but I think it was sealed already.

It was terrible confusion then. We were all trying to organize a line of Homeward Bounders to stop *Them* dropping off. He was towering off one

way, and Konstam was at the other side. I shoved
Helen off to hold down another end. I could see her
arm blazing all through. I tried to organize my end,
but most of the Homeward Bounders were so mad to
get at *Them* that they wouldn't stay there. I had to do
most of it myself. In a way, it was easy. I had only to
go near *Them* to have *Them* recoil from me in horror.
But I couldn't risk getting too near for fear *They*
would get unreal enough to escape into the spirit
world or somewhere—anyway, get too unreal to be
killed. I think I could have snuffed all *Them* I came
to out with just a touch, but that would have been
cheating. I was the odd one out and I couldn't even
kill one of *Them*. I knew that if I cheated in any way,
They would take advantage of it in time to come. So
all I could do was run up and down my end swearing
and shouting, and trying to herd *Them* into the fight
in the middle of the Place. And *They* realized. *They*
began to come at me in a body.

I was in real trouble, when a boat drove up
against the empty edge beside me. It was a black
haggard boat with torn sails and flying ropes, and
covered with barnacles. Its skinny, hollow-eyed
crew looked like a set of monkeys. The one at their
head looked more human, because of his coat and his
seaboots. He was waving a curved knife—a cutlass
maybe—and the monkeys had the same sort of
knives in their shaggy mouths.

"Hello!" I shouted, as they all came swarming

down into the Real Place. "Flying Dutchman! Help me hold *Them* back!" And I shouted to them what was going on.

The Dutchman grinned at me. "One each is not forbidden, eh? Kill twice? A pleasure."

After that, they strung out in a line and not one of *Them* got by. I stood with them staring at the terrible muddled battle, in and out and over the tables. *They* cheated all the time. I suppose *They* were desperate, but it didn't make it any better the way *They* rolled machines on Homeward Bounders and squashed them. *They* would attack people who were trying to keep the rule, or push one of *Them* at someone who had already killed one, so that they had to fight back in self-defense. The two monkeys next to me both killed one and a half of *Them* that way. And that meant that *They* could attack the monkeys. After a bit, I don't think anyone knew who had kept the rule and who hadn't. Except me. I dared not cheat. And there were people like Ahasuerus, who didn't care after a bit. Ahasuerus got one of *Them* who was crouching over this machine I'm talking into. I was shouting to him to come over and help the monkeys, when one of *Them* went for somebody small just behind the machine — it looked like Adam — and Ahasuerus got that one too, in the nick of time. Afterwards he held his hands up in the air and shouted in despair, and after that he just didn't care anymore. He ran amok. He was terrifying.

It was over in the end. There were humped people and humped gray shapes all over the Place, and just a huddle of *Them* left alive in the middle. *They* had known there would be. I went to look at what the one talking into the machine had been saying, and it said,

The rules are on our side. There will be enough left of us to and Ahasuerus got him then.

Konstam rounded up all of *Them* in the middle and respectfully asked him Helen called Uquar what to do with *Them*.

"You'll have to send *Them* over the edge," he said.

So we did that, shouting and waving, like driving cows, with me in the middle to keep *Them* scared. The edge was a lot nearer by this time.

After that there was a time for meeting before going Home. He—the one I set free—seemed to have no trouble understanding the machines. He found a machine that sent people Home. And he told me how to work this one I'm using. But that was later. At that time, he was away in the middle of the Place helping people get to the right worlds. He said now that *They* were gone, even the oldest of them could go Home and settle down in peace. I found Helen and Joris and Adam rushing up to me. Konstam and Vanessa were on their way over too, but they stopped on the way for a passionate hug. I was right about them.

"Jamie, which world is yours?" said Joris. "Are

you going there now?"

"It's the same as Adam's," I said. "And no, I'm not."

Of course they all shouted out, "Why *not*?"

"Because I'm a good hundred years too late for it," I said.

"So that's why you said it was like yours!" said Adam. "I see! But you can come and live with us, Jamie. I know it won't matter."

"And be like Fred?" I said. "No, it won't do, Adam. You've got too many rules and regulations there now. I should never get used to them. You need to be born to them."

Vanessa and Konstam had come over by this time. They stood with their arms round one another, looking at me. I was sitting on one of the game tables. A little world was still going on underneath me, but nobody in it knew. "Are you sure, Jamie?" Vanessa said.

"Yup," I said. "You'll never believe this, Vanessa. I'm your great-great uncle."

"Good Lord!" she said. She saw things quicker than most people. "Then you won't go Home with Adam."

Joris said eagerly, "Then you can come with us!"

"I'd like to pay you a visit," I said. "I want to meet both the Elsa Khans."

Konstam began to see, I think. "Just for a visit?" he said. "You could stay for good."

"Just a visit once in a while," I said.

"Then you'll have to come to the House of Uquar with me," Helen said, as if it was settled. "You can help me turn my world back into a good place again. It'll be fun."

I only wished it was settled. "I'll visit you too, Helen," I said. "I promise."

That made her furious. "Then I shan't ask you!"

I told you Adam was quick at understanding things. He said, "You're going to go on being a Homeward Bounder. Why? I've only been one for a fortnight, and I hated every minute."

"Ah, but I've got the habit," I said. I didn't really want to explain how it was.

"Nonsense," said Vanessa. "There's something more to it. *Why*, Jamie?"

And they all kept at me, until I said, "It's a matter of this Real Place, you see. *They* got it and got to be able to play *Their* games by anchoring it down, sort of, first with him over there, then with Homeward Bounders. As long as we all believed there was a Real Place called Home, and as long as he knew he was going to get free in the end, *They* had this Place. And all the worlds were not so real. But now that's all gone, and he's free and the worlds can be real again, we need an anchor for that too. If we don't have one, *They* can have a Real Place again. And I'm the anchor."

Helen turned straight round and stormed off to where he was standing high among a crowd of people waiting to be sent Home. I could see her haranguing him fiercely. No kneeling this time. A lot of yelling instead. I saw him ask the people to wait a moment. Then he came over to us with Helen.

"You're right about the anchor," he said to me, "but it doesn't have to be you."

"Who's better than me?" I said. "I'm still young. I may be a hundred and twelve years old, but I've got hundreds more ahead of me. And you said yourself that no worlds are real to me. You were right there. I think it has to be me. Don't you?"

"I'm afraid I do," he said. I thought Helen was going to bite him.

"Rather you than me, Jamie!" Adam said.

That was about it, really. They got used to the idea, and then we hung about talking. Joris gave me his clock-thing so that I could find the Bounds. That would have been difficult without *Them* making moves any longer. I was grateful for that.

When the Place had got quite a bit smaller and all the others had gone, he came over and said they ought to be going Home too. I went over to the sender with them to say good-bye. That got a bit difficult. And then it got worse, because when Adam was all set to go, Vanessa said, with a beaming smile, "I'm not coming. I'm going with Konstam."

"Yes, you go alone, Adam," Konstam said, ever so happy.

"Oh no!" I said. They turned and glared at me. Who was I to forbid the banns? "No you don't!" I said. "You go Home first, Vanessa. You go with her,

Konstam, and ask her hand in marriage, or whatever people do these days. But you're to tell her parents. They'll understand. I talked to them a while ago and I know how they're feeling." And, when Konstam stared at me with his head up, full of the pride of the Khans, I said, "Look, whippersnapper, I'm four times your age, and I know what's best. So."

That made Konstam laugh. "Very well," he said. "Joris, do you mind going on your own for now? Tell Elsa Khan I shall be bringing Vanessa as soon as I can. And tell her we can get to work and exterminate all the demons now, because *They* won't be stopping us."

So all three of them went, and then Joris. When it was Helen's turn to go, I suddenly found an elephant's trunk wrapped round my neck again. "Now, now! You don't drag me off again so easy," I said.

"Not if you promise to visit me *soon*," Helen said.

"Very soon. Next after the Khans," I said.

"Why them first?" she snapped.

"Because the chief of *Them* came from that world," I said. "I don't want *Them* roosting there."

"All right," she said, and unwrapped the trunk and went.

That left only him and me. We wandered about the silent shrinking Place for a while, he telling me all the things I wanted to know. And he made me promise to visit him again soon too. Oh, I have friends to drop in on, all right.

Then he left. I think he hated it in *Their* Place, even if he didn't hate *Them*. It was good of him to stay so long. And that left only me, talking into this jabbering machine. It's beginning to jabber a bit slowly now. I have to stop and wait for the hopping bit to catch up with what I'm saying all the time. The machines here are all running down as the reality goes, just as he told me they would. But the Place hasn't got much smaller now for some time. That means I have to be going too.

You see how it works, do you? As long as I don't stay anywhere long, as long as I keep moving and don't think of anywhere as Home, I shall act as an anchor to keep all the worlds real. And that will keep *Them* out. Funny kind of anchor that has to keep moving. It's going to go on for such years too. I shall grow old in the end, but it's going to take a long, long time. The more I move, the longer it'll take. So I shall have to move because of that too. I'm going to keep *Them* out as long as I can.

The bit that I'm going to hate is the first part, when I go and see Helen. Every time I go, she's going to be older than me. There's going to be a time when I shall still be about thirteen, and she'll be an old, old woman. I shall hate that. Still, I promised. And at least I shan't be in any danger of thinking of Helen's world as Home. Nobody could, except Helen.

If you like, you can all think of it as my gift to you. I never had much else to give. You can get on and play your own lives as you like, while I just keep moving. This story of it all can be another gift. I've made an arrangement with Adam. When I've finished, which is almost now, I'm going to put the bundle of papers in the garden of the Old Fort, before I move on. Adam's going to get them and take them to his father. And if you read it and don't believe it's real, so much the better. It will make another safeguard against *Them*.

But you wouldn't believe how lonely you get.